A House of Tailors

A House of Tailors

patricia reilly giff

WENDY
LAMB
BOOKS

Published by
Wendy Lamb Books
an imprint of
Random House Children's Books
a division of Random House, Inc.
New York

Wendy Lamb Books is a trademark of Random House, Inc.

Visit us on the Web! www.randomhouse.com/kids
Educators and librarians, for a variety of teaching tools, visit us at
www.randomhouse.com/teachers

Library of Congress Cataloging-in-Publication Data

Giff, Patricia Reilly.
A house of tailors / Patricia Reilly Giff.
p. cm.
Summary: When thirteen-year-old Dina emigrates from Germany to America in
1871, her only wish is to return home as soon as she can, but as the months
pass and she survives a multitude of hardships living with her uncle and
his young wife and baby, she finds herself thinking of Brooklyn as her home.
ISBN 0-385-73066-7 (hardcover) — ISBN 0-385-90879-2 (library binding)
[1. Emigration and immigration—Fiction. 2. German-Americans—Fiction.
3. Sewing—Fiction. 4. Uncles—Fiction. 5. Brooklyn (New York, N.Y.)—
History—19th century—Fiction.] I. Title.
PZ7 . G3626Hr 2004
[Fic]—dc22   2003026103

The text of this book is set in 12-point Bauer Bodoni.

Book design by Kenny Holcomb

Printed in the United States of America

October 2004

10 9 8 7 6 5 4 3 2 1

BVG

in memory of

Christina Schütz Schaeffer,
Katharina Schütz,
and the Uncle,
Lucas Traschütz

Thank you to my dear editor, Wendy Lamb, who is always there to encourage and advise . . .

to Kathy Winsor Bohlman of the Westport Library, who cheerfully, and expertly, finds the answers to my many questions . . .

and, as always, to St. Jim, my dear children, and my grandchildren, who read and critique and make life worth living.

Breisach, Germany

1870

one

Outside was war. I could hear the pop-pop-pop of the cannons.

Inside was the sewing room. Gray cloth forms of Mama's clients stood along one wall, reminding me of the soldiers we saw on the streets outside, but without their spiked helmets, of course, or their splendid blue tunics with the gold trim.

War! How exciting it was. Our own German soldiers from the Fifth Infantry Regiment had swarmed into our sleepy little town, determined to take on the French who lived just on the other side of the Rhine River.

And that sparkling river flowed so close to our front door I could have tossed a stone from my window and seen the ripples it made in the water.

I didn't care two pins about our Otto von Bismarck

and his determination to unite all of Germany in this war. What difference could it possibly make to me?

But I did love to think about those soldiers, who looked so fierce and elegant . . . and who wandered up and down the street so close to the sewing room that I was tempted to tap on the window with my thimble and wave to them.

Mama would have had a fit!

Being a soldier would certainly be better than sitting here in this room sewing buttons on Frau Ottlinger's winter bodice—ten brass buttons from collar to waist—running the thread through the tallow to give it strength.

Frau Ottlinger, Mama's most important client, thought she was going to be a fashion plate this Christmas, dressed in the style of those infantrymen. She was more likely to look like a breakfast bun studded with raisins.

"Dina!" Mama said. Even with her back turned she knew my mind was wandering. And I knew exactly what she was going to say next: "Christmas is almost upon us, and we have dozens of orders still to fill!" As she spoke, she rubbed the already spotless sewing machine wheel with a soft cloth.

That sewing machine! It was like a cranky member of the family that had to be cleaned, and polished, and fed with oil whenever I turned around. And every two minutes it seemed we had to put a new piece of felt underneath to save the rose rug from being worn away.

Today there was a fire in the grate, and smoky lanterns for light—smoky because I had forgotten to wash them. Mama had swished the curtains closed in anger at the first burst of gunfire. "These dresses must be finished tonight," she had said to my sister, Katharina, and me. "Pay no attention to those ruffians out there."

Anyone who disturbed Mama was a ruffian.

Luckily the curtains were opened the width of one of Mama's business cards: *Frau Kirk and Daughters— Tailors*. I could see part of our little southern German town of Breisach nestled between the mountains and the river, and once in a while a cannon flash as our soldiers fired across that river at the French.

France would be defeated, we knew that. Someone had told Mama the French had no harnesses for their horses, no bullets, and, worse, they were fighting smallpox, a disease so terrible it made me shiver to think about it.

Poor Elise, my French friend for so many years. She lived on the other side of the river, and we had met at a fall festival in happier times, when we were less than ten years old. How often on early sunny mornings we rowed back and forth across the river to trade patterns, and cookies, and gossip.

Mama leaned over me now. "Those buttonholes look like cabbage heads."

I looked down guiltily.

Mama took the bodice and my needle. Carefully she made invisible blanket stitches around the edges of the top hole, filling in the space to make it smaller. "You know how to do this as well as I do." She patted my shoulder. "You are thirteen years old. Stop dreaming. We have no time for it."

Stop dreaming. Stop thinking. I stretched my

cramped fingers. I remembered the first buttonholes I had made at the age of four, practicing on a piece of toweling, first Mama, then Katharina showing me patiently. How many buttonholes had I made since then? A thousand?

Mama was sympathetic. "I know it takes forever to do all those buttons when you'd rather be—"

Reading the letter that's propped up on the fabric table was what I wanted to say. "Having morning muffins," I said instead so that I wouldn't be accused of having more curiosity than König, our cat.

My eyes kept going to the letter that had arrived this morning: a tissue-thin envelope covered with stamps from America. Mama had said, "I'm too busy adding the braid to Frau Ottlinger's skirt to open it. It has nothing to do with you anyway, Dina." But she smiled to take the sting out of her words.

And my older sister, Katharina! She didn't have as much curiosity as the piece of tailor's chalk on the table. With barely a glance at the letter, she had picked up a package of flannel sheets, neatly hemmed, and gone out the back door to deliver them to a family on Mettau Street.

I was on the fifth button, holes newly drawn in, when at last Mama stood up, arching her back and running her hands over her waist as she left the sewing room for the kitchen. I'd have about three minutes alone while she stirred the soup and added the marrow balls she had prepared an hour ago.

Out of my chair in an instant, I picked up the letter, which crackled in my hand, and tried to read the words through the envelope.

In my mind was a picture of the uncle who had sent

it: Mama's rich older brother, who lived in luxury. No wonder! Everyone who lived in Brooklyn, New York, probably did. After his first wife died, he had married again and sailed immediately for America. How romantic it was. I hadn't seen him since I was a little girl, but I imagined him handsome and funny, and the young second wife, Barbara, slim and lovely.

I held the letter up, turning it one way and then another. The name *Katharina* jumped out at me. "Katharina," I said aloud. "What is he saying about Katharina?"

And I was caught, of course.

Mama plucked the letter from my hand.

"Well, what do you *think* it says?" I asked.

"I know what it's about," Mama said, "and Katharina does, too."

"Why don't I know? Why is it that everything is kept from me?"

Mama shook her head impatiently. "Nothing can be kept from you for very long." She sighed. "My brother is offering Katharina a place with him and his wife."

I sank down on the chair, my heart thumping in my chest. "And I? Will I go with her?"

Mama shook her head. I could see she felt a little sorry for me. "Only Katharina."

Katharina to go to America! I loved my older sister; she was my best friend. Katharina to go, and not me?

Katharina to go!

I would never see her again. Never. Not unless somehow I could go, too, years from now. We'd be old. And even though Mama's brother and sister were there, Mama had never thought of going. "My home is here," she had said. My eyes burned. *Dear sister gone forever.*

Mama picked up Frau Ottlinger's bodice. In fine thread she began to stitch under the collar: *Frau Kirk and Daughters.*

"Why do you bother with that?" Bitterness rose in my throat as I thought about Katharina going away, even though I knew how selfish I was. After all, it had been Katharina's dream first. How many times had I heard her talk about the great world across the sea! But to stay here without her! Bent over a piece of fabric, a needle in my hand, for the rest of my life!

"My name?" Mama asked. "Because I'm proud of our work. That's the most important detail for me."

I had my own dreams of America. Hadn't I pored over the pictures of New York I'd found in a magazine: elegant women with their hair clipped back behind their dainty ears, wearing hats with feathers and ribbons that dipped down over their eyes? Hadn't I turned the pages to see ladies wearing faille gowns in the great ballrooms of Madison Avenue?

And wasn't I the one who had studied all those English words: *Monday* and *Tuesday, March* and *May, come* and *go, this* and *that?*

I thought of the Uncle then, and Barbara; I thought of Aunt Ida, Mama's sister, who was the cook in a great house. Soon she would go west and live on the prairie with her husband, Uncle Peder. Why couldn't I go to America, too? That huge young country across the ocean. I said it aloud: "Mama, why not?"

Mama took the letter from my hand and tucked it

into her belt. She sat down and picked up the coil of braid, taking several stitches before she answered. "There is more than one reason, Dina," she said around a row of pins in her mouth.

"But what?"

"First, he didn't ask for you."

I bent over Frau Ottlinger's buttons. What could I say?

"And even if he had," Mama said, looking at the large dark portrait over the sofa, "I have money enough for only one passage, and that has taken years to get together."

Papa's portrait. I knew she was thinking of him and how little we had to spare now that he was gone.

The cathedral bells began to toll: twelve, almost lunchtime. My younger brothers, Franz and Friedrich, were playing on the stairs, pounding each step in time with the bells.

Those bells always reminded me of Papa with his soft beard and great dark eyes; Papa, who bent down and listened to each of us sympathetically. I closed my eyes, remembering the day the bells had announced the arrival of the new bishop. Papa, the master lock- smith in our village, had opened the great cathedral door with the gold key he had made for the occa- sion . . . and allowed Katharina and me to hide in the choir loft to see the ceremony.

If only he were here, still alive, he would under- stand how much I wanted to go to America, how much I hated sewing.

I thought of a night two years before, misty with rain. Papa had gone out for a walk, returning to cough and cough. He had died days later as we sat at his bed-side, Mama saying, "His throat was always weak. Always!"

How different everything would be if he were still here, I thought. *Oh, Papa, I miss you!* Without thinking I ran the needle into my finger and quickly sucked the stab of pain away.

Mama finished the last of Frau Ottlinger's braid before she spoke again. She took the scissors that hung from a loop around her neck and carefully snipped the thread.

"Sometimes in life there are no choices, Dina," she said. "It's hard, but sometimes it's easier than having too many choices."

Before I could say anything the front door opened. It was Katharina back from Mettau Street. Mama's eyes were on me. I brushed my tears away and took a deep breath, ready to tell Katharina how happy I was for her.

Two

The bed was warm. I could see the flicker of the gaslights outside, so it was still early, too early to think about getting up. I turned over, the letter still on my mind. Mama had finally read it aloud last night, and it was just as she had said.

"We have room for Katharina," Uncle Lucas had written. "She will have her own room. From what you have written over the years, she is quiet and helpful. . . ."

Her own room. What would that be like, I wondered, not having to share a bed, stretching both arms from one side to the other? I saw it in my mind: shelves in the cabinet to spread out my petticoats, my stockings, my gloves; my hat perched on a shelf all by itself.

If only the uncle had added one more sentence.

We have room for Dina, too.

If.

Mama always strung happenings together with that

word, reminding me of the garnet necklace she looped around her neck every morning.

"Don't you see, Dina?" Mama had said one day last month, tapping one thin finger gently on my wrist. "If you hadn't forgotten the bread rising on the stove . . . if you hadn't banged out the door with enough noise to wake the dead . . . then you wouldn't have bumped into Frau Ottlinger with enough force to send her flying off into the street.

"And—" Katharina had barely held back her laughter—"if the street hadn't been clear of carriages at that very moment, Frau Ottlinger would have been run over by a horse."

"Ah, no," Franz had said, nudging Friedrich. "Frau Ottlinger would have run over the horse."

Friedrich had nearly fallen off the kitchen chair laughing, but Mama had tapped harder. "That's not the point. The point is I nearly lost Frau Ottlinger as a client, and I did lose the bread. When it came out of the oven, holes the size of your fist ran through it."

I turned over in bed again, punching my pillow, thinking of another day sewing for Mama's clients, threading needles; running fine stitches in and out of the silk, the linen, the wool; working on seams, and darts, and plackets.

And then I remembered. I sat up straight and slid out of bed in one motion. How could I have forgotten what my plan was for this morning? Still I hesitated. What I was going to do was so simple. Usually so easy. But now so dangerous.

Next to me, Katharina slept on like the dead, her dark hair covering her closed eyes with their long straight lashes . . . camel eyelashes, I called them.

I twisted my hair up on the back of my head, then opened the door quietly, a pair of old shoes in my hand.

The second-floor stairs couldn't fool me. The top steps were quiet, as they should be. It was only when I reached the ninth and tenth squeaky treads that I had to watch out.

With both hands I put my weight on the banister. I glided over the next two steps on my bare toes, *plink plink*, and raced to the bottom.

Safe.

Mama slept on; so did Katharina. Franz and Friedrich were probably awake, fighting in their bedroom. But what did they care about what I was doing?

Outside the hall window I could see the great Cathedral of St. Stephen, and in front, the river with its thin spirals of early-morning mist.

I tiptoed into the sewing room and pulled on a pair of Papa's old pants from the drawer—so old I could see the large uneven stitches I had made in the waist when I was beginning to tailor.

What would Mama say if she caught me wearing trousers? I couldn't imagine. But the last time I had done this, my skirt had been muddied, almost ruined. I had had the worst time hiding it from her.

I sat down on the slipper chair to squeeze my feet into worn shoes with cracked leather. I didn't dare wear good shoes for what I was about to do.

At this hour of the morning the forms of Mama's clients looked like ghosts without heads, arms, or legs, waiting to have fabric draped over them, pinned, and sewed. In the center was the form of Frau Ottlinger, our richest client, but certainly not the thinnest.

Frau Ottlinger and I had something in common: we both loved wide noodles, and coffee cake for dessert. And when I knelt on the floor to pin up her hem, she'd wink at me. "Put the candy plate a little closer on the serving table, Dina," she'd say. "We don't want it to fall off, do we?"

But never mind that now. As soon as the six o'clock bells sounded, Mama would be out of her bed, and Katharina, too. I rooted through the drawers for the pattern I was looking for; then, back in the hall, I opened the door. König, our cat, padded out ahead of me, and I stepped outside myself. It was chilly, but there was no going back for a wrap.

"Dina." The voice came from above. Franz was leaning out the window still in his nightshirt.

"Shhh," I called up. "Go back to sleep."

"I want to come with you to see the soldiers."

Heaven! Mama would collapse if she heard that. "I'm not going to see the soldiers," I whispered as loudly as I dared. I motioned for him to close the window. "Want to fall out?"

I looked to be sure no one was in the street, then crossed the walk with König and slid down the bank of the river, out of Franz's sight, out of Mama's hearing.

The river was beautiful in the morning, peaceful. I knew this time of day well. Many times I had rowed across to the French side to talk with my friend Elise, and to exchange patterns. What did we care that we were on opposite sides of the war!

Mama and Katharina talked endlessly about the war: Otto von Bismarck's North Germany linking up with us in the south to create one country to fight against the French. And now the infantry was going to take Fort Mortimer away from the French, then their castle at Neuf Breisach, and move on to the castle in Belfort. But Elise and I didn't talk about any of this; we tried not to think about it.

Next to the stone wall that kept the river inside its boundaries lay an abandoned skiff. I had used it many times. As the river began to capture the rosy sunrise, I slid into the skiff and began to pole my way across. I knew Elise would be waiting for me.

I glanced back at the cathedral that towered over our town. Soldiers were there, our own German soldiers, in the bell tower, using that height to watch the fort on the French side. Soldiers in such a holy place!

I thought about going back, but Elise wanted my dress pattern as much as I wanted the new French design for a hat that she had promised me.

I saw her waving and nudged the skiff onto the landing. "A little wet, this pattern," I said apologetically.

"You must go right back," she said, handing me the hat pattern, made of thin paper with its cuts and arrows, and directions in French.

We hugged for one quick moment; then I was on my way back. I could see myself wearing the most elegant hat in Breisach on Christmas morning.

And then I thought . . . there was something I could do for Katharina. I took a breath. I could make the hat for her.

Mama had a saying: *As much as you hate sewing, Dina, that's how much the needle and thread love you.*

I knew it was true. We all knew. For some reason,

my stitches were straight and true, my seams almost invisible. I could cut into the fabric almost without using a pattern. Yes, as hard as it would be to give up making it for myself, Katharina would have that hat. I'd keep it a secret until the very last moment.

Even as I thought it, I had to swallow. I comforted myself with the thought of the hat I had made earlier, my beautiful hat that I had copied from a picture of one worn by Elizabeth of Austria.

Frau Ottlinger *coveted* that hat. But even Mama shook her head. "It is Dina's, and it is not for sale."

But the new hat, even more wonderful, I would surely give to Katharina.

So busy was I daydreaming, I didn't look up until the skiff bumped into our side of the river. I barely heard the heavy boots sliding down the bank toward me, and by that time it was too late.

It was one of our own soldiers! His rough hand covered my mouth. He was so close I could smell the onions on his rank breath. I fought him, feeling my hair caught in the buttons of his tunic. "French spy," he said.

I couldn't shake my head, couldn't answer. He stepped back and I was pulled along with him, up the riverbank to the street, where König stood guard over a poor dead mouse.

Three

I could feel the mud against the heels of my shoes as the soldier dragged me along the river promenade.

How could this be happening?

The windows of my house were across the way. If I had one second to scream, my family would be at those windows, Mama and Katharina, Franz and Friedrich, and in the next second, they'd be outside to help me. If only Papa were alive. He'd make short work of this soldier.

I did see Frau Ottlinger in her window several doors down, handkerchief to her mouth, just staring as I was pulled along.

I tried to raise my arm to plead for her help, but then we were past her window, and she had seemed frozen.

We went along the narrow path near the bridge, and I could feel the soldier's grip loosen. I pulled forward, strands of my hair ripping from my scalp, and turned to make my escape.

But I had gone only a few steps when I ran full tilt into another soldier: the same brass buttons, the same blue tunic. But this one had a stiff mustache and beard, and mean narrow eyes, and he raised me high up, my feet in the air.

"A spy," the first soldier said. "I saw her pole across the river from the tower. I saw her exchange—" He held out his hand for the pattern that was tucked in my sleeve.

"You see," he said, smoothing out the paper on the top of a stone. "French writing, arrows for direction . . ."

"Her?" asked the other one. "Her?" He looked at Papa's trousers as he set me down in front of him, so close I was only an inch away from that terrible face, those accusing eyes.

My heart was pounding, the pulse in my throat beating so fast and so loudly I felt as I had that time years before when I had leaned too far over the edge of the bridge and fallen into the river. The sound of the water had filled my ears, a giant underwater echo. With my hair covering my face and my clothing weighing me down, I had gone deep below the surface. It had seemed forever until Papa had pulled me out, gasping and vomiting water.

Now there was no Papa to save me. One soldier stood in back of me and the other in front. "It's a pattern for a hat," I told him, trying to catch my breath. "I'm not a spy, not French. I am as German as you are."

"She watches to see our movements," one told the other. "How many we are, where we are going."

"We were just exchanging patterns." I was babbling now. A shopkeeper came along the path, and when he saw the soldiers he hesitated, then backed away.

The soldiers didn't believe me. And even to my own ears my story sounded strange. Who would cross the river to the French side while we were at war?

Who but a spy? Or someone like me!

I could hear Mama's voice in my ear. *If you hadn't sneaked out . . .*

If.

And at that moment, the pattern was caught by the wind. It sailed over the stone wall and into the river. It floated on the ripples and sank just beneath the surface of the water.

A third soldier came toward us. This one was a little younger than the others, maybe Katharina's age. He had a small fencing scar on his cheek and his eyes were as blue as the sky overhead.

"Please," I began.

"A spy," the first one said at once. "She'll have to be tried, but the outcome . . ."

"Shot," said the other.

"Oh no," said the blue-eyed soldier. "You must be wrong. She's just a girl."

"Trousers," said the first. "What girl would ever—"

Behind us came the noise of a cannon. It was muffled and must have been close to Wolfgantzen, but it was enough to make the first two soldiers turn like a pair of geese to see what was happening.

When they did, I ran. Ran faster than I ever had before, trying to decide which way to go. The shops were to my right, still closed and locked, and I'd have to go to the end of this street before I could get to the next. But to my left was the narrow road climbing to the Kaiserstuhl, a volcanic outcrop that hovered high over Breisach.

I passed the statue in the square with the fountain

trickling water and began to climb the hill. The two soldiers were behind me, one of them shouting, "Sooner or later we'll find you, and when we do, you will be charged." Only the third, the one with the clear blue eyes, said, "Let her go. A girl, only a girl."

It was a steep path, but no one knew it better than I. Its rocks, its tree roots waited for the unwary, and the soldiers were unwary. Here I had luck. Often I climbed the narrow path that wound around the hill.

I left them far behind.

By the time they decided to give up I was in a sheltered corner of rock, bending with my hands on my knees to breathe normally once more.

I stayed for hours looking down on the river with its boats and barges, a bright ribbon spooling through the countries of Europe, wending its way to the sea. What would Mama and Katharina be thinking? I wondered. How worried they must be!

And I? More frightened than I had ever been in my life. Sooner or later they would find me.

It was almost dark before I crept down that long twisting path, heart leaping at every sound. At the last turn, I could see Katharina below me, pulling her shawl close around her shoulders, rushing back and forth in the narrow streets like a little hen, searching for me.

Dear Katharina.

I navigated the rest of the way as quickly as I could, not daring to call out to her, trying to make myself invisible as I crossed the square.

And then she was in back of me, almost pushing me into the house, whispering frantically. "Frau Ottlinger saw you and the soldiers and ran to tell us. I've been wandering around all day looking for you."

four

The heavy drapes in the sewing room were tightly drawn. Covered with dried mud, I sat in front of the table, my face filthy. Surrounded by the forms and the shelves filled with spools of thread and packets of ribbon, Mama and Katharina paced . . . from the window to the sewing machine to the chairs against the walls. Katharina clenched her hands tightly together as she and Mama tried to decide what to do about me.

Friedrich and Franz sat on the bottom step in the hall peering in at me, probably glad they had stayed home in bed this morning.

This morning! Such a long time ago.

I kept whispering how sorry I was in between Mama's "If only . . ." and Katharina's "You could have been shot by our own soldiers!"

Soon Frau Ottlinger slipped in the front door. Usually dressed so carefully, now she looked disheveled, her hair poking up as she ran her fingers through it. "Dina," she said. "What have you done?"

"It was only a pattern," I began.

"That soldier," she said. "He swears that you are a spy." She fanned her face with her hand. "I told him you didn't live in Breisach, that I had never seen you before."

"Suppose the soldiers come here?" Friedrich asked.

There was silence. "How can we keep her hidden?" Mama said at last, and began to cry.

Katharina seized the Uncle's letter and looked at Mama.

"Oh, Katharina," Mama said.

"It can't be helped," she answered.

I looked from one to the other, then reached out to Katharina. "What are you thinking?"

"You will go to America instead of me."

Frau Ottlinger nodded slowly. "Yes, that's the thing to do. Of course."

I shook my head. "Do you think I would do that to you? Never."

Katharina knelt down next to me, smoothing my hair, then pressing my hands in hers. "We can't take a chance. You must leave before they find you."

Mama was already nodding, and before I could say a word they were scurrying around, pulling out the old trunk, rushing past each other on the stairs with folded clothing and Mama's best shawl. Mama thrust a sturdy skirt into my hand: "To wear on the trip."

And Frau Ottlinger hurried home to ask her husband to drive me to Freiburg within an hour.

Freiburg. To my grandmother's house.

"You'll stay there until the passage is arranged."

Mama sighed. "From there to Hamburg and then a ship."

If I had been brave, I would have given myself up to the soldiers. Instead, I bowed my head over the skirt, my tears dripping on the cloth, ashamed of what I had done.

For the first time I realized how much I loved this house and the river. How terrible it would be never to hear Friedrich and Franz laughing and playing on the stairs. And Mama!

But the worst was Katharina. How could I leave and know I would never see her again? How had I not thought about this before?

Katharina bent over the trunk, her eyes on the ceiling. "Soft fabrics to bring for Barbara's baby, and ribbons." She reached up, pulling yards of pink silk off the shelf.

I changed my clothes and then sat there, numb, looking around at the room I would never see again, and then at my brothers. They'd grow up, become men, and I wouldn't be there to see them. How well would they remember me . . . their sister who left when they were so young?

And then the hour was gone. The trunk was filled and closed, waiting in the hall. Mama cupped my face in her hands. "Will you write every week?" she asked.

I nodded, unable to speak.

"I'm not much of a letter writer," she said, "but I'll try. And I'll think of you every day for the rest of my life. Know that, Dina."

My brothers, solemn for once, stood on the step, looking the way they had when Papa died.

I said goodbye to Katharina in the hallway. She

emptied her pocket. "Take this," she said, handing me her treasure, a small envelope of buttons Papa had carved the year before he died.

At the last moment, I ran up the stairs to get my Sunday hat. I brought it down to Katharina. "I want you to have this." How bitter I felt. I loved this hat, but because I was greedy to make an even better one, I had deprived Katharina of her right to go to America. Now she would be the one to stay, and I to leave.

She held it in her hands, turning it, looking down at it. "You are the best of us, Dina."

I closed my eyes. "I won't have to sew again," I said, trying to smile. "Not in America."

And then we were holding each other, hugging each other, until Friedrich said, "Herr Ottlinger is here."

We broke apart and I went down the front steps without looking back.

Brooklyn, New York

1871

five

I angled for a place near the railing of the ferry, stepping around packages of every shape I could imagine and through knots of people, practicing my English: "I beg you parrdon."

They paid no attention. All of them were talking and pointing to the shore, so close we could almost reach out and touch it. I felt as if I could almost grasp a chunk of soil in my hand.

Was I the only one alone? I glanced at a family over my shoulder, two children clutching their mother's skirt and another in his father's strong arms, his small fingers tangled in the man's beard.

I stood there shivering, tucking my hands into my sleeves. Who knew what had happened to my gloves on this long journey? But never mind. It was almost over.

After leaving Breisach, I had stayed in Freiburg at my grandmother's house. I had waited there for days until my cousin Karl could take me as far as Hamburg, where they had arranged passage for me. I had crossed that ocean alone on a miserable ship; fifty-seven days it had taken!

Now there was only this last bit, the ferry from Castle Garden to the dock. I had gotten through all of it. I was a world away from home and my family.

Again I was reminded of something I had thought of so many times: Katharina guiding me across the great stone bridge over the Rhine, holding my hand. I must have been only four or five years old. She had hoisted me up so that I could see a passing barge that left a smooth white V in the river, and we waved to the pilot in his ribboned hat and striped jersey.

"Someday, Dina," she had said, "I will sail on a ship a hundred times the size of that barge and go to America. I will walk along Madison Square and have dinner in the Fifth Avenue Hotel like in the picture over our bed."

I could see her in a hat with ribbons blowing in the breeze. "I will go to America, too," I had said.

Oh, Katharina.

Leaning against the railing now, I saw buildings on each side of the water. They weren't nearly as grand as the ones that lined the river at home, I thought uneasily. There were no castles, no great bridges.

I closed my eyes, remembering that storm that had come up out of nowhere on the trip.

That Friday morning the waves had been flat, and it seemed we were skating across a huge pond. By afternoon, it was as if a madman stirred the ocean with a giant spoon, creating waves that were high enough to cover the ship.

And the wind! That gigantic wind. Trunks slid and

people screamed, but I couldn't hear them, only saw their open mouths. It was the wind I heard, circling over us, around us, a hundred times louder than the train that thundered down the tracks along my river.

With Papa's Bible in both hands, I promised God that if I lived through this storm, if I ever put my two feet on land, I'd never eat a morsel of food or wet my mouth with a drop of water on Good Friday again. I would keep that promise; I knew I would, even if I lived to be an old woman.

Now in back of me on the ferry was a family from Frankfurt. I caught bits of their conversation, their long wait on the stairs, shivering with cold and fear, to see the doctor at Castle Garden, the examination of their eyes when he rolled back the lids with a buttonhook.

A buttonhook!

I never wanted to think of that examination again. How the doctors had poked and prodded while I stood there, almost numb with embarrassment, wondering if they were going to chalk my coat with an X and send me straight back across the ocean.

But I didn't want to think about where I had come from, either, Mama standing in the doorway, one hand to her throat, tears streaming down her cheeks. The boys. Katharina. I felt a choking in my throat.

I wiped my eyes with one hand, wondering why the thought of coming to America had so excited me in the first place.

The ferry was close now, and people's faces on the dock became distinct, some of them smiling, some looking anxious as they waved to us.

I searched those faces, remembering the Uncle as I had seen him years before. But there were so many people packed together in a mass, and so much noise. Some of the voices spoke German. "Here, Glenda, look here!" "Peter. Darling . . . I'm over here."

The boat hit the dock with a screech and an enormous crash, and I nearly lost my balance. I straightened my hat . . . and there below me was the Uncle, looking older than I remembered. He was tall and straight, his hair gray now under his hat, his beard trimmed, his scarf blowing against his cheek.

At that moment the gangplanks were lowered, and people began to stream off the ferry like the beans Mama funneled from their canvas bag into her pot.

The Uncle motioned to me to wait.

I could do that, couldn't I? Wait for one minute while everyone else raced down to the dock, waving their arms, or pushing trunks and wicker baskets? I could wait to see this rich land, the Uncle's beautiful house, Barbara, his wife.

The Uncle had written Mama that he worked for a woman with so much money that when meat was ordered, the butcher stood on the scale with the side of beef and charged for both weights.

Suddenly I was wild with excitement. I raised my hand to wave, thinking of the needles that had stabbed my fingers every day since I was four, the hours in front of that sewing machine, running up seams, turning collars, binding blankets and sheets.

No more! I would never sew again. Well, a rip in the seam of my skirt or a hole in the toe of my stocking. I almost hugged myself with joy. Never mind the soldiers who looked for me, or my dear river, or the cathedral bells that tolled away the hours. I was in America!

six

At last it was my turn to go down the gangplank. I tried to remember what Mama had told me about being a lady, about being correct. But I ran the last few steps, my hat skimming off my head and sailing down on my back, held only by the woolen ties against my neck.

I ran straight into the Uncle's arms.

He was surprised—no, more than surprised. He was shocked.

I stepped back. "I'm here," I said a little uncertainly. I raised one shoulder in a half shrug. "Me instead of Katharina."

"I see that." He didn't smile. "Wait until I bring your trunk."

I stood there, waiting forever, it seemed, watching the sea of people around me and the foaming wake as the ferry began its trip back to Castle Garden, until he returned carrying my trunk on his shoulder. We began the walk to my new home.

I remembered the last time the Uncle had come to Breisach. I couldn't have been more than five, sewing a bit of lace on my doll Gretchen's coat.

"You will be a good tailor like Uncle Lucas," Mama had said.

"Wait." He had picked up the tiny coat. "You do it like this, the lace underneath so the stitches don't show."

I had pulled it back. "No, like this. It's my doll, my doll's coat, my lace."

I wondered if he was remembering the same thing. How could I have forgotten that even then we rubbed each other like emery? Was he disappointed not to have Katharina there? Katharina, who was quiet and soothing, and never in trouble.

I swallowed. The Uncle had been right about the lace, of course. But what was I thinking of? Sewing had no place in my life from this moment on.

I chattered to him all the way, ignoring the cold gray day. "Katharina sent soft cloth for the baby, Maria," I said. "Barbara can run up nightgowns and shirts. And there's pink flannel, the softest pink for a blanket, and rolls of ribbons, rose and green. I will embroider roses and leaves on the binding for her myself."

I stopped. Had I said that? But what was a little embroidery for a baby? I couldn't count that as sewing, not at all.

It was a long walk through the streets, and several times the Uncle stopped to shift my trunk from one shoulder to another. But I didn't mind the distance at all. I stared at the stone houses, one attached to the next, like the ones in my own city.

There was a difference, though: the streets were filthy. Every time we turned a corner, I expected to see the houses become grander, the streets cleaner. But when we finally reached the last corner and the Uncle put down the trunk once more, and pointed, I saw our house.

I drew in my breath. Such a tall house. True, there were droppings from the horses in the streets, and bits of coal and sawdust that rose up in eddies and settled again as a rogue wind turned them from one direction to another. But the size of this house!

Would I have one floor all to myself?

By the time we entered the vestibule I knew I was mistaken. "The top floor is ours," the Uncle said.

Only the top?

My heart fell, but I told myself it was all right. I didn't need a whole floor; all I needed was a bedroom of my own.

We began the climb. I followed the Uncle up the stairs, holding on to the broad wooden railing, breathless as we navigated the steps and the stairwells.

One woman peeked out of a doorway and nodded at us, her head covered with a kerchief, a broom in her hand. And on the next floor was a girl who looked almost like Katharina. She smiled at me shyly before she closed the door again.

On the top floor, the door was open, and Barbara stood there, beautiful and slim, just as I had pictured her, and so tiny she didn't quite reach the top of my head. She waited for us, arms out.

I flew into those arms, hugging her, and was surprised to notice the lovely smell of cinnamon. In back of her was Aunt Ida, Mama's older sister, looking so like Mama, except that her cheeks were round and full, her arms straining at her sleeves. She covered my face with kisses, patting my cheeks with soft, plump hands. "Ah, Dina, Margarete's daughter."

And Barbara said, "Look, Dina, a surprise for you."

Propped up on the sewing machine at the other end of the hall was a letter. I recognized Katharina's handwriting. But the other thing I noticed made my heart lurch inside my chest, my breath almost stop. I looked at the red patterned carpet, at the machine with a chair in front of it . . .

. . . and underneath the machine, the rug was worn bare, almost all the way through to the floor. Worse than our rug!

In that second, I knew this was a house of tailors, no different from my own, except that it was poorer.

"You sew," I blurted out.

The Uncle blinked. "Of course I sew. Every minute I can when I'm not working for Mrs. Koch."

I took a step backward. I tried not to act shocked. Where had I ever gotten the idea that people who lived in Brooklyn were all rich?

What had I done? I asked myself. What had I done?

15 January 1871

Dear Dina,

    I am sending this letter on even though it may reach Brooklyn ahead of you. I like to think it will greet you when you arrive. How much we miss you! There seems to be a hole at the dinner table. No one to laugh with, no one to tease, no one to reach for second and third helpings.

    First the news of the war.

    After the French lost Fort Mortimer and then the castle at Neuf Breisach, the soldiers left our town. They went on to lay siege to the French fortress at Belfort, but that fortress held out, still holds out.

    A soldier returned, asking questions about you in the shops. It must have been that terrible soldier who followed you that day. Even though no one answered him, it seems he is determined to find you. How glad I am that you are far away and safe.

    But there was one unusual happening, Dina. Do you remember a third soldier? His name is Krist. He has a fencing scar and blue eyes almost like Papa's. Somehow he found out that you lived here. Don't worry. He came to see if you were all right. He has no use for the two soldiers who chased you, but he's glad that you are far away and safe.

    You'll know that Mama was very impressed with him when I tell you that every time he comes, she puts out her best tea set.

    Krist. Isn't that an interesting name?

    Dear Dina, I send hugs and kisses. Franz and Friedrich cry for you.

Your loving sister,
Katharina

And on the bottom in Mama's heavy script:

    Dearest child, how much we all miss you! Grandmother said you were very helpful. I hope you will be helpful to Barbara, too.

Love,
Mother

seven

From the time I reached Brooklyn I longed for warm weather. I thought it would be like Breisach—sunny, with a cool breeze from the river. But when the heat came, long before it would have at home, I was shocked. My arms were prisoners in their sleeves; my back almost sizzled on the roof of the house.

By that time, the tin roof was my bedroom!

I could no longer sleep in the closet that had been fitted out for me. That first night the Uncle had opened a door off the hall and said, "Your room." I looked in at a pantry meant to store bags of flour, and tea, and sugar. "I have taken everything out for you. Barbara and I have cleaned." He waited for my reaction as if it were a chamber for Elizabeth of Austria. "Room for your trunk at the side of the bed," he said, as if he had thought of everything.

I swallowed. Barbara had tried, I knew that. A crocheted spread covered the tiny bed, and a starched white towel with embroidery along the edges lay at the foot.

The spread was exactly like the one on Mama's bed. They must have shared the pattern. I ran my hand over it, wondering if I would disgrace myself by crying. "It's lovely," I managed. "Really lovely."

"You can close the door, Dina," Barbara had said. "You will have privacy that way." Still, she looked worried. A thin line appeared between her eyebrows, and she smoothed down her apron as, behind her, Maria pulled on the strings until she untied the bow.

"Thank you, dear Barbara." I made myself smile, and I could see the relief in her eyes.

The Uncle clapped his hands together. "How you worry for nothing," he told her.

But later, when I closed the door and sat on the edge of the bed, I felt as if I might suffocate without light and air and a window to see down into the street.

I ate so much at that first dinner, too much: a huge piece of brisket, a high pile of noodles I quickly devoured, pickles, and salad! What a festive dinner, with bread pudding Aunt Ida had made for dessert. Aunt Ida, who had been here since I was a baby, the first of the family to come to America. She had fallen in love with a man who was determined to see the world.

After a while I folded back the spread and opened the trunk with its pink lining, which Mama had sewed in quickly that last afternoon. I began my first weekly letter home.

I wrote about Barbara, who kept a whole cinnamon stick in her pocket. I wrote about the funny things Maria did, how she refused to have her shoes buckled and her curly hair combed, how she pushed food off her wooden high chair and watched the crumbs fall around our feet. Maria the tyrant, Barbara called her. I wrote about everything I could think of except what was really on my mind: home.

When I was ready for bed, I said my prayers. I didn't know how they should go. I said, *Thank you for the safe ending to my journey;* but then, *Dear God, if I could only go home again.*

And I closed my eyes.

There was a trick to falling asleep: relaxing my muscles, letting my hands go limp and my thoughts come easily.

Hadn't I used that trick every night of my life without even realizing it?

But this night it didn't work. I turned one way and then another. I told myself to stop thinking. I clenched and unclenched my hands.

At last I crept out of my tiny room and up to the roof. That first night it was too cold to sleep there, so I walked back and forth, my arms crossed across my chest, in an agony of homesickness, until I was weary enough to go downstairs and sleep.

After that it became a habit to go to the roof to think about my new family: Barbara, her hair falling into her face as she leaned over the stove; Maria, who made me laugh with her terrible temper; the Uncle . . . What did I think about the Uncle? Silent most of the time, smiling only when he looked at Barbara or Maria, spending every spare moment at the sewing machine.

And then in no time the heat reached Brooklyn. Every night I tiptoed up to that tin roof with my pillow, ducking under the limp wash that hung on lines crisscrossing almost every inch of space.

One night, always a special night at home in Breisach, I stood in a corner of the roof, holding on to the ledge, and looked down at the houses, the streets where heat shimmered up at me. I'd been too embarrassed to mention it was my birthday, so not one person here knew about it. There was no one to whip up a birthday cake, to tuck a small present under my pillow.

I watched people who sat on their steps or on the curbs, trying to escape the heat. Dray horses clopped up and down the streets. Insects buzzed.

What would Katharina think of this place?

I sank down on the roof, cushioning my head in my arms as stinging insects rose in a cloud above my head. They were worse than the heat tonight, crawling under my collar and through my hair. When I moved, they darted up angrily and swooped down again to pierce the soft skin around my eyes, and the lobes of my ears, and under my chin.

I raised my hand to my face to slap at one of those devils and saw the smears of blood they left on my fingers and the edge of my sleeve. I didn't even know what they were called, but their high whining sound kept me from drifting off.

I *had* to sleep. A pale rim of pink was already reflected in the windowpanes of the houses across the way.

In the apartment downstairs, Maria began to cry. I didn't blame her. She was covered with prickly heat and welts from those insects. Through the open window came Barbara's voice, singing an old lullaby. The cries became softer, Barbara's voice trailed off, and then there was silence.

How often had Mama sung that song?

Don't think about it, I told myself. *Don't think*

about Mama's face. But that was all I could think of, night after night, Mama with her smooth hair tucked into a loop at her neck, her pale skin with faint lines around her eyes, those eyes always sad since Papa had died. Mama shaking her head. *Oh, Dina. What have you done this time? If only . . .*

And now for the rest of my life I would be here, with no way back to Mama and Katharina, to my brothers.

My eyes were so swollen from the insects and from crying I could hardly shut them. But at last they closed. I fell asleep with my thoughts chasing themselves. How would I get home? How could I get the money? I'd have to find a way.

I knew it would take years, but by then the war would be over and the soldiers long gone. I would save every cent, store it in a roll of stockings the way Mama did. When I had enough, I'd travel back to Breisach.

I woke to a red ball of sun far to the east. The day was going to be even warmer than the night before.

eight

Everything changed that morning.

It began at breakfast. I helped Barbara lay out the cheese, the rolls, the thick cups, and poured the coffee and milk into pitchers.

How different it was from our breakfasts at home, with Franz and Friedrich spilling things and laughing, and Katharina good-naturedly wiping up after them.

Here everyone was quiet, with just the sounds of knives and spoons clinking and Maria banging her wooden blocks on her high chair.

It might have been because the Uncle looked exhausted, almost too tired to eat. He worked hard, I had to admit that. First he spent a long day working for Mrs. Koch. And then after a late dinner he sat at the sewing machine running off five or six skirts, or pairs of trousers, or shirtwaists for Mr. Eis, who sold them in a shop in Manhattan.

But that morning, the Uncle cleared his throat. "It's time for you to work, Dina."

Barbara shook her head. "She's helping wonderfully, Lucas. Didn't she make that roast last night, and she's cleaning. . . ."

"Yes." I agreed with him instantly. "I need money. I could go out and . . ." I tried to think of what I could do.

But that wasn't what he had in mind. "Right here," he said, waving his arm toward the sewing machine. "It is a busy time for tailoring."

I brought the cup of coffee to my mouth. It almost scalded my lips.

Late summer at home. Waking up in the dark to hem heavy skirts, to turn over cuffs, to shape collars. Not stopping for meals, but gulping down vegetable soup that Mama stirred and then poured, running back and forth from the kitchen. Every hour the cathedral bells tolled, reminding us that coats, suits, and dresses had to be ready for the clients at a moment's notice.

I swallowed that first burning sip of coffee before I looked up at the Uncle, thinking carefully of what to say. "I want to do something instead of sewing." My words were even, as if I weren't challenging him, but I could feel the pulse at my throat, the slight trembling of my fingers against the cup.

The Uncle raised his eyebrows. "And what, may I ask, can you do?"

I put the cup down before I could spill it. I couldn't look at him.

He stabbed a piece of cheese from the platter with his fork and stopped to chew. "Katharina would have gone into service."

I leaned forward. "Service?"

"We would have found a place for her at Mrs. Koch's house with Ida. She would have become a maid there, doing some cleaning, and maybe a little cooking."

"I can—" I began.

"You can't," he said. "You're too young."

"Only four years younger," I said, as if it were four months. "Besides, I'm not going to sew."

Barbara stood up quietly and took Maria out of the high chair. In a moment both of them had disappeared down the hall and into the bedroom.

"You are fourteen," the Uncle said. "You need food and a place to stay." He leaned forward. "Do you think I can afford to have even one person in this house who doesn't work?"

Sounds came through the open window: a horse clopping, someone calling. It must have been almost a hundred degrees in that room. I could feel perspiration on my forehead, my back. But at the same time I was chilled.

"If you will send me back to Breisach," I said, "I will return the money someday."

"If you want to go back, write to your mother. I have no money to spare."

I bit my lip, telling myself that not one tear would drop from my eyes. I put on my *I don't care* face, which used to drive Katharina wild.

"You can sew well. I know that. Your mother is so proud of you. The best of all of us, she says." His face was red. "Today you will clean the sewing machine," he said. "There's oil in the closet." He waved his hand vaguely toward the kitchen counter. "And now I must go to work. *Work*." He almost shouted the word.

He stood up fast. The plates on the table rattled; his cup wobbled, spilling hot coffee across the table.

I sat there, my hands shaking under the table as he jammed his hat on his head and stamped down the stairs . . . *boom boom boom*. I could hear every step of each flight.

And then that terrible bang as he slammed the door on his way out. It must have startled everyone in the building.

There was no help for it. I had just exchanged one sewing machine for another. And this one was much older than the one in our sewing room. I had to say, though, that the Uncle kept it carefully; still, he did so much sewing at night with so little time to clean, it was covered with lint.

I bent over it just as I used to at home, using a small brush to dust out the fluff, and then squirted oil on a cloth to go over the works. When I was finished, it fairly shone. The belts that turned the wheel were black and slippery; the metal reflected my face.

But this wasn't even a sewing room. Nails were beaten into the hall wall to hold the large spools of thread. Folds of cloth were stacked on the floor so that I had to take huge steps around or over them.

Barbara tried to explain. "Poor Lucas," she said. "All he wants is his own shop, a place to put things, a place to spread himself out, a place where he can do what he loves."

"Sewing?" I said. "He loves sewing?"

She nodded. "Yes." And as she said it, her face turned the color of the river after a storm. She rushed past me to be sick in a basin in the bedroom.

A baby, I thought. She was going to have a second

baby. I would be sure to tell Mama and Katharina in my next letter home.

Maria was out of her high chair now, holding a roll with butter and jam, smearing it on the floor and laughing.

I had to laugh, too, running my fingers over her arms and under her neck. "Mouse fingers," I said. But all the time I was thinking about the Uncle.

I had just lost my first battle with him. It wouldn't be the last one I'd lose.

nine

Barbara and I bumped the baby carriage down the stairs to the outside steps. "How hard you've worked all morning." She smiled at me. "We deserve time for a walk."

She had worked hard, too, lugging water from the outside hall to the kitchen, washing Maria's diaper cloths and the Uncle's work shirts, then going to the roof to hang them.

But now that she was having a baby, I told myself that from today on I'd be the one to carry up that heavy wet wash.

I took a breath. How hot it was! Too hot to do anything but sink down on the stoop. Everyone else had the same idea. All along the street women sat outside fanning themselves and their babies with paper. And as I looked up, I could see more of them leaning out the windows on pillows, calling back and forth to each other. Children darted between wagons whose drivers called, "Iceman, fresh ice. Get your ice," and "Rags. We buy and sell. Any length," and "Knife sharpener here."

The smell of dirt from the horses and rotten fruit was everywhere.

I had brought dresses with me from Breisach, all wool, and the one I wore today was heavy and clung to my legs. My stockings were wool, too. But I had found a packet of pale pink cotton under the stacks of cloth in the hall, and uncle or no uncle, with Barbara's blessing I had begun a dress for myself. I had seen a great spool of cotton thread as well, and would knit a pair of stockings as soon as I had time.

I felt my chin go up as we crossed the street. One thing I knew: I was going back to Breisach. And to do that I had to get money for the passage.

Barbara was talking, telling me that she had money.

I jumped, startled. "Will you give it to me?" I asked. "My mother has very little money. But I promise you I'll send it back as soon as I can earn it at home."

She put her hand on my arm. "Enough money for a cup of ice cream, Dina," she said. "In this heat . . ."

I did cry then. As I walked along, with my face turned so Barbara wouldn't see, tears dripped from my cheeks onto the wool dress with its heavy buttons, a river of tears.

I hated the Uncle; I hated Brooklyn with its sun beating down on my head and on its streets so that everything smelled. And now we were in a shopping area where the butchers' doors were open and the smell of great sides of beef wafted out to us. Sheep carcasses hung on hooks, and pig heads were jammed one after another into the windows. Some of them had sprigs of green in their open dead mouths.

It made me want to gag.

"It's hard to leave home. I remember how I felt when I first came here." We walked in silence then. Barbara put her hand on my arm. "Aunt Ida is homesick, too, but for a place she's never seen. She longs for the prairie, for a small house with her husband. She's working, saving, so she can join him."

I told myself I could do that, too. Work and save. Someday I'd go home to Breisach.

Sitting on an iron bench in a park, Barbara and I shared a paper cup filled with shavings of ice drizzled with lemon syrup. I had never tasted anything so good. It filled my mouth with its tartness and slid down my throat, leaving a trail of icy coldness. Even Maria was smiling as Barbara held the cup out to her to suck.

A breeze lifted the leaves of the trees, the park was green, and I felt as if I could breathe again. As I sat there, I made my plans. I wouldn't argue with the Uncle; it would get me nowhere. I'd sew for him at night, doing the finishing work on the skirts and shirtwaists as he ran up the long seams on the machine: a bit of braid here and there, buttons sewed on in a moment, as Mama would say, "with a red-hot needle and a burning thread."

But during the day he had to let me go into service. I was big for my age, a good worker. No one would know how old I was. And that money, at least that money, would be mine.

I tried to count in my head. Who knew what that

would be in American money? I shut my eyes, frowning. A fortune, that much I knew.

"What is it?" Barbara asked.

I felt my eyes well up again, but I brushed at them angrily. No more crying. If it took years, then years it would be.

A thin line of perspiration trailed down the side of Barbara's forehead; moisture dotted her upper lip. "Let me take the baby," I said. "Just rest here a few minutes, and I'll walk with her."

I pushed the carriage around the park, looking up at the heavy green branches. Suddenly I was startled by the snuffling of a horse. I jumped, and the two men on the seat of the wagon in the street next to me laughed. They were big men with long dark beards and were a little frightening.

I started to turn away, but before I did, Maria waved to them, a backward wave that she was just learning. It looked almost as if she were waving to herself. "Hey, little girl," one of them said, waving back, and smiling at her. "You look like my daughter."

I took another turn around the park and went back to Barbara. "Did you see those men?" she asked. "The ones in the wagon?"

"Maria waved," I said.

"They're from the health department," she said. "Searching out cases of smallpox."

Smallpox. A shiver went through me even in that heat. I remembered stories from home: in the French army across the Rhine River, the disease went from one soldier to another. Men raged with fever, their faces ruined with pockmarks; many of them died.

Barbara put her hand on my arm. "Don't be afraid," she said, looking fearful herself. "We'll put red ribbons in the apartment. That's supposed to bring luck against it."

We stood up and began to walk again, past a group of houses with shops on the ground floors: a gift shop with cards and flowers wilting in the heat, an empty store with the windows dark and black, a man in black sewing at a table below a sign in the window reading MENSWEAR.

I pointed it out to Barbara. "That's what we need," I said. "A proper shop with shelves to hold the fabric and thread. Drawers to hold the patterns." I took a breath. "At home—" And then I found I couldn't finish.

But Barbara didn't notice. "You sound like Lucas," she said. "That's what he wants. All he wants."

I pressed my lips together. I wouldn't talk about our sewing room at home with the windows that over-looked the river.

Barbara pointed. "That's the Schaeffer family's shop. They tailor men's clothes. Suits and trousers."

Through the window I could see more than one machine, a woman finishing hems, a man bent over running up a seam, and a boy about my age sewing buttons. He brought the fabric with the button attached up to his mouth and clipped the thread with his teeth.

I opened my own mouth in a little O. A tailor should know better. I could hear Mama's voice. *A bad habit, bad for the teeth, bad for the thread. Use the scissors, Dina.*

The boy saw me watching him.

Quickly I turned away, but before I did, I saw him wink at me.

My face flushed. What would Papa have said to
that?

I went back to the apartment thinking about the
boy's face—a plain face, but friendly. How nice it
would be to have a friend, even if it was just a boy who
didn't know how to sew buttons onto a shirt! And
when I opened the door I was happier, because there in
the hall, waiting for me, was an envelope addressed to
me in Katharina's neat handwriting. It must have
taken weeks to get to me. Still, I ran my hand over it,
knowing that Katharina and Mama had touched it.

2 May 1871

Dear Dina,

*I have so many things to tell you. I wore your hat to
Sunday services. Frau Ottlinger has offered once more to
buy it, but I will never sell it to her. "It is Dina's hat," I told
her, "just in my safekeeping."*

*I enclose a new hat pattern. Elise managed to send this
with someone who dropped it at our door. She thinks you
are still here, and sends love. A beautiful pattern, isn't it? I
studied it carefully. It's worn down over the face like one of
Mama's dinner crepes. Lace puffs up in back and a single
rose is tucked in the center. Too bad it's straw, that's so
hard to work with, but I just heard of a new machine that
will sew straw. Can you imagine?*

*The war is over. We heard that the fortress at Belfort
held out for one hundred eight days . . . even after Paris
signed the peace agreement. Isn't that amazing? Both
armies were so impressed that they left Belfort where it belonged on the French side instead of annexing it as they did
Alsace and Lorraine.*

*All these months later, I am tortured by the thought that
we might have hidden you somewhere closer. But I was surprised to see that soldier lounging in the square, and felt a
deep stab of fear.*

I'm sure we have done the right thing.

Friedrich and Franz are growing every day. Both are learning how to sew. And Frau Ottlinger misses you. She says you both love lemon cookies. Mama doesn't make them anymore. She says it makes her miss you more.

Krist and I talk about you, and together we wonder what you are doing. Krist remembers you as a brave girl, as brave as the French soldiers who fought against our soldiers at Belfort. I remember you that way, too.

Love,
Katharina

Dear Child,

I must tell you I never even realized how much sewing you did for us. I don't mean the seaming and the pressing and the turning of collars. I mean the odd things, if I may say odd: the seed pearls on a cuff that you'd decide to do on a whim, the extra bands of lace sewn into a sleeve.

Ah, Dina, I send you hugs.

Love,
Mama

Ten

That night I had my second argument with the Uncle, even fiercer than the first.

I was reminded of the Prussian and French soldiers with their grim faces and smoking guns. How well I remembered that morning on the bridge with the two soldiers, especially the one with the beard and the terrible eyes. But, thinking of Katharina's letter, I told myself I must not act like a weak little girl without a brain. I was fighting for a way to get back to my home in Breisach someday, and I couldn't afford to be afraid of anything. Especially not the Uncle.

At dinner he told us about his day washing Mrs. Koch's carriage, her horses, and even the barn in back of her huge house, where they were kept. Dark shadows lay in crescents under his eyes, and the frown lines in his forehead seemed deeper than they had that morning.

I waited until dinner was over and Barbara had

gone back to the bedroom with Maria before I spoke. "Are you ready to see the sewing machine, Uncle?"

Katharina would have told him to watch out. "Like König the cat, Dina has claws that you don't see until you've been scratched," she had said once when I had bested her in an argument.

I followed the Uncle down the hall and watched as he inspected the machine. He spent time running his fingers over the belts, and moved the needle up and down to see that it went smoothly. "Dina can sew while I am at Mrs. Koch's house," he muttered to himself. "Barbara will keep the house and help in between. It will work; yes, it will work."

Even though he tried not to show it, I could see he was impressed with the way the machine gleamed in the flickering light.

Why not? It looked like new. And I had begun to organize the fabric he had managed to buy for the time when he had his own shop. I had refolded the pieces so they lay against the molding in neat piles, the heaviest at the bottom, the lightest at the top, matching colors where I could.

"I will sew for you at night." I narrowed my eyes just a little, the way I did at home when Franz and Friedrich were bothering me. "I can sew quickly when I need to, but my stitches remain tiny and even and well placed."

"What are you talking about?" he asked. "What do you mean, at night?"

I took a breath. "I mean to go into service with you and Aunt Ida during the day."

His face reddened. "You will work all day and then come home to take a few stitches for me?"

I raised my chin. "More than a few."

He was frowning, the lines in his forehead a wash-board. "You will sew for me during the day. There is lots of work to do here, jackets and skirts and shirt-waists."

My lower lip went out. "I have a pattern for a hat," I said. "From Paris." I didn't say it was made of straw. I didn't say how impossible it would be to do.

The flicker in his eyes matched the gaslight.

I rushed on. "I know the hats they are wearing in Paris and Breisach this year. I know what I need to make them and how to shape them."

I drew myself up. I'd always been tall for my age, but still I came only to his shoulders. "Half the women in Breisach are wearing my hats and I'm only fourteen years old."

Not quite the truth. In my mind I could see Mama's eyebrows raised almost to her hairline, and I looked up quickly to see . . . something. I wasn't sure, but was he ready to laugh? It was almost as if he could guess the truth. I *had* made hats once, for Frau Ottlinger and both her daughters, but nothing like the one I had made for myself, which by some miracle had turned out so well. Even I had been able to see that the rib-bons that hung down the Ottlingers' backs were a lit-tle crooked as I sat behind them in church.

I *had* made two other hats after that, and they had sold. They were better, though the flowers were heavy in front and sparse in back.

As I was thinking of Mama and home and bending over those flowers to secure them to the felt, the Uncle be-gan to pound his fist on the edge of the sewing machine.

If he had been about to laugh, he wasn't laughing

now. "Do you think you can come here and tell me how important you are?" he asked.

Bang.

"Anyone can see you are just a child."

Bang.

"A child who eats more than the rest of us."

Bang.

"Two pork cutlets at supper. Two helpings of creamed potatoes, two of carrots."

Bang.

His hand must have hurt. He stopped pounding and covered his head with both hands.

I had an enormous appetite, it was true. Once, at home, it had been my turn to chop the carrots for the stew. By the time I had finished cutting, I had eaten almost all of them.

For a brief moment I almost felt sorry for the Uncle. He had hoped for dear, good Katharina and had gotten me instead.

I slid onto the chair in front of the machine and ran my hands over it. "I can easily sew for you at night. I don't need much sleep. And most of my work is by hand. You can use the machine while I sit at the kitchen table."

In my mind, I saw Mama raise her eyebrows again. By the time the cathedral bells tolled nine times every evening, I was yawning. By ten o'clock, I was tucked up in my third-floor bedroom so sound asleep that Katharina had trouble pushing me to my side of the bed to make enough room for herself.

The Uncle's neck looked as if it were too big for his stiff collar. He seemed as if he might explode.

I pulled a spool of pink thread off its nail on the wall so that I wouldn't have to look at him, looped it under and over the machine hooks, and in one swift movement threaded it through the needle.

"What are you doing?" he asked.

"With all this work you want me to do," I said, leaning over to reach for the pink flowered cotton on top of the pile, "I will need a dress that won't suffocate me."

"I will take it out of your wages when you go into service," he said.

"That's fair."

"Fair? You think any of this is fair?" He marched down the hall and slammed the outside door so hard I could see the fabric trembling under my fingers.

I rubbed my hands on the wool of my skirt. They were damp. And my heart was still pounding.

But I had won, hadn't I? I calmed myself by taking deep breaths as I went back into my airless bedroom to pull a simple dress pattern out of my suitcase.

Kneeling on the hall floor, I pinned the pattern to the fabric and cut it quickly, thinking how glad I was that Mama had filled the bottom of my suitcase with starched white collars and cuffs.

I stood up, rubbing my back. What an endless day this had been.

It was much later by the time I sat in front of the machine, my feet on the treadle, and fed the material under the needle. I started by sewing the three pieces of the bodice together, matching the tiny flowers so it was impossible to see where they had been pieced, and then I gathered the sleeves into their openings.

By the time I began the four long seams of the skirt, I was hungry again. I told myself that I could do without, but I could hear the ice dripping into the pan under the icebox. I knew there was one small cutlet left on a plate.

I went into the kitchen and sprinkled a little salt onto the cutlet. Then I leaned against the windowsill. People below were still sitting on the steps to keep cool. I was getting used to the look of them: an old man reading a newspaper, a knot of women talking to each other, and even children playing in the dark streets. I closed my eyes and took a bite of the cutlet.

eleven

While I waited to hear if there was a place for me, I sewed during the day, or helped Barbara, who grew more tired each day. A few times I walked past Schaeffer's Tailor Shop to see what the boy was doing. Most of the time he was staring out the window. I wondered if he hated sewing as much as I did.

One afternoon I returned from my walk, went into the hall, and began to pin the pattern to the fabric the Uncle had left for me.

Hideous, the whole thing: pattern, thread, and brown fabric.

Horrible thick material. Who would buy such a jacket? And what would they pay?

As the sun poured in through the side window, I sat there cutting, changing, then marking in darts with tailor's chalk, to give a little shape to this poor piece of work.

And all the while I thought about that pattern Katharina had sent me. The hat dipping down over the eyes, the lace. How it would look in church on Sunday. And another thought. The boy in the tailor shop. He had been in church last Sunday.

I couldn't make a hat from straw, but something kept tugging at my brain. I stood up and stretched, wiping my hands on the sides of my skirt. There wasn't a breath of air in that hall. Not a breath of air in Brooklyn. And poor Barbara was downstairs on the steps trying to keep Maria happy.

I wandered into the kitchen and poured another cup of water from the pitcher.

And then that little tug at my brain pulled everything into focus. Instead of straw I could use . . .

What could I use?

A piece of cardboard, perhaps, covered with . . .

Not one piece of fabric in the hall was possible. The Uncle had no idea of style.

I pictured Mama bent over the trunk before I left, her hair falling over her eyes as she tucked the pink fabric around the insides. "At least this," she had said, patting the edge of the trunk, and sewing it carefully. A pink hat would be perfect with the new cotton dress. I could do without a lining in my trunk very well.

And then I was moving through the kitchen, opening drawers, going back to my bedroom, searching for . . .

And there it was, the bottom drawer of my dresser. I stood there thinking about it, Mama frowning in my mind, Katharina's horrified face.

The bottom drawer wasn't made of wood; it was nothing but a thick piece of cardboard.

What would the Uncle say to my hacking the cardboard away from the wood?

What would poor patient Barbara think?

Even so, I was back at the machine pulling out the large scissors, scissors that certainly would need sharpening after I was through with them.

Another picture of Mama in my head, saying, "A tailor is only as good as his scissors and thread."

But never mind that. I stabbed at the inside of the drawer, the dresser groaning and trembling as if it were alive.

When I was finished, I knelt on the floor to draw a circle on the heavy piece of cardboard, then cut it out. I plopped it over my head and stood up to see myself in the dresser mirror.

I could cover this with the pink lining, cut petals from the pink fabric, and dye them a deep rose.

I dropped the circle on the dresser, thinking it was a wonderful plan, a perfect plan, and while I was congratulating myself, there was a tremendous bang on the door. The health department men were there, coming into the house, down the hall, looking into the kitchen, the bedroom, to make sure we harbored no one sick with smallpox.

I drew myself up. "We are healthy," I said. "Don't you worry about that."

And later, to make a perfect day, the Uncle came home and told me that Aunt Ida had a place for me at Mrs. Koch's house. I was to replace a helper who had left for the West.

Dear Dina,

I write this on your birthday, dear sister. We have not forgotten you! I think of you all the time, but I have given up the idea of coming to America. Don't feel sad for me, Dina; it was just a childhood dream. I have taken down the picture of the Fifth Avenue Hotel and Madison Square and have given it to Friedrich. Perhaps he will go to America someday.

But now the really important news. With Mama's permission, Krist has given me a ring. We will be married in September. Such a few words, but my heart is beating with excitement as I write them. You can see now why it's possible to give up my lovely dream.

Hugs and kisses,
Katharina

Dina dear,

I add this quickly so Katharina won't see. Do you remember the lace handkerchief you made for me? With your permission I will add Katharina's initials and yours for her to carry on her wedding day. She is so happy, Dina, smiling often, singing. And I approve of her choice. Krist is a good man, loyal and upstanding.

Happy birthday and love,
M.

Twelve

Katharina to carry my handkerchief! I remembered the day I had found the perfect pieces of lace to sew around the fine lawn fabric. Thinking of her wedding made me happy even though I wouldn't be there. I pictured her as a bride. Together we had sewed many wedding dresses . . .

But now I had to pay attention to the Uncle's mutterings as we walked toward Mrs. Koch's house.

"How is this going to work?" he was saying, as if I weren't there. "She can't even speak a word of English." He took long steps so it was hard for me to catch up.

"I know *pliz*," I said, trying to keep my new skirt out of the dusty street. "I know *tenkyou*."

He stopped and waited for me to catch up. *"Please,"* he said in such a loud voice a woman ahead of us turned around to see what was the matter with him. "And *thank you.*"

To me it sounded as if there weren't any difference, but I said the words under my breath all the way to Mrs. Koch's house. I knew more than those two, of course. I knew at least a dozen words, *door* and *stairs* and *greenhorn*, which was what the iceman had called me yesterday, and *izecrim*, which was now not only my favorite word—I loved the sound of it—but my favorite food as well.

And *Fifth Avenue Hotel*. I knew those sad words now. It made me think of Katharina's dream that was gone. And here I was in America, and I had never seen that hotel myself.

The Uncle looked at me. "That hat."

I raised my hand to my head. The hat was a disappointment. The cardboard wasn't stiff enough, so the sides curved down under the weight of the lace and ribbon.

"And I thought . . . ," the Uncle said.

I raised my chin.

He sighed. "You are not a hat maker, I can see that."

We turned the corner. It was clear that this was the best street in Brooklyn! It wasn't that the houses were so different—they were still made of the same brown stone—but the steps were higher and wrought-iron gates were everywhere. Even the horses in the street looked elegant. They had been brushed until they gleamed, and were attached to carriages that waited for their owners to step outside.

Carriages with velvet seats!

I whooshed up the steps of the house in back of the Uncle, pretending I lived there and the horse belonged to me. What would I name him?

"Pay attention," the Uncle said as he pulled the knob of the doorbell.

In a moment, Aunt Ida was in front of us, round in her long white apron. I thought again that she looked like Mama except that she ate much more. I could sympathize. I was hungry already and I had just finished breakfast.

"Ah, Dina." She pulled me inside, glancing up at the great stairs that led to the second floor, shooing the Uncle toward the back of the house with three fingers, and whisking me down one flight into her kitchen.

The kitchen was as large as the Uncle's house.

Aunt Ida smiled at my hat with its droopy edges, took it off, and placed it on a shelf. She straightened my collar, then reached for a starched apron on a hook. She twirled me around, tying the apron strings around my neck and yanking gently at the ones down at the bottom. "Later," she said, "you can tie those, too. Pull up your dress to form a little bustle over them and it will be easier to work without falling all over your skirt."

Next she poured me a coffee mixed with condensed milk and slid a plate of toasted bread over to me. And all the time she was talking, asking about Breisach and the Rhine River—my river—and Mama, and Katharina, and the boys, clicking her tongue over poor Papa, whom we would never see again.

I slid onto a high stool, watching her prepare a breakfast tray, while I took bites of the buttery bread that melted in my mouth, and sips of the sweet coffee.

"Mrs. Koch came from nearby at home," she said. "Heidelberg."

I had been there once, a small bit of a town tucked in the mountains.

"She came here with her husband," Aunt Ida said.

"They worked hard, so hard, at horse training." She leaned over to take a nibble of the bread. "And now they are rich." She paused and leaned forward. "Are you homesick?"

Homesick. I felt a terrible longing for home in my chest. Even if I saved all I earned, it would take years before I'd see my river again.

But I wasn't going to tell Aunt Ida anything about my plans to go home again. I wasn't going to tell anyone.

I gave a quick shake of my head, and by that time Aunt Ida was telling me about herself. "I work hard, too." She swept her hands around to show me the immaculate kitchen. "Someday soon there will be enough money for me to join Peder out west."

"How long ago . . . ," I began.

"Two years, long years," she said. "But he is building a house for us and tilling the land. And soon I will bring money for a cow and some hens." She shut her eyes tightly. "I will take the train from Manhattan at Varick Street, a long ride, out to the fields and the hills. . . ."

A bell was ringing somewhere upstairs, and Aunt Ida handed me a tray. "Take this up. Can you manage? Knock on the door with one hand. Don't drop it. . . ." She wiped her hands on a towel. "Top of the second set of stairs."

She took three or four steps behind me, tying the bottom strings of the apron and pulling my skirt through so I had room to walk, and up I went with the tray, up two flights of red carpet with fat blue blossoms.

The tray was filled with more of the buttery bread, a pot of coffee, and a pitcher of cream. There were two little bowls, one filled with raspberry jam and the other with marmalade, that made my mouth water. They slid back and forth on the tray as I took the turn in the stairway.

I was so busy thinking about all the good things on the tray that I forgot to knock but opened the door with my elbow, just glad to have arrived with everything still in one piece.

No one was there.

I slid the tray onto a round table in the center of the room, wiped up a little marmalade that had spilled onto the tray with my apron, and wondered what to do next. Call out?

The Uncle was right. I didn't even know the English word for breakfast. As I tried to decide what to do next, I saw hatboxes piled up on the shelves in back of the half-open door to the closet. The boxes themselves were tied with ribbon and bunches of lily of the valley. They were so beautiful I could only imagine what the hats inside must look like. My fingers itched to lift the lids.

If only I had a dust cloth, I could dust my way into the closet before the woman came back for her breakfast.

I tiptoed to the hall door and poked out my head. Everything was quiet. I looked at the thick red rug with its fat roses that went on forever, the closed doors on each side, four altogether, painted a shiny brown.

I went back to the tray. A shame about the toasted bread. It would be cold by the time the woman ate it. I removed a tiny blob of raspberry jam from the rim of its little bowl with my finger and slid it into my mouth.

I could have eaten everything on the tray myself in about two minutes.

Instead, I went into the closet, closed the door in back of me, and stood there taking in that wonderful space, as large as my bedroom at the Uncle's house. A framed mirror hung on one wall, almost like the one in Mama's living room, but this one was much larger, with more gilt and a baby angel flying on top.

I leaned close to the mirror. Good thing. I could see a dab of raspberry jam in the corner of my mouth and quickly licked it off. What would Mrs. Koch or Aunt Ida say? It would be hard to explain that I had been neatening up the tray.

I wondered if I dared to open one of the hatboxes, but then I saw that two of them were open on the back shelf, the tops leaning back against the wall.

I reached up and pulled the nearest box off the shelf, still listening for the sound of the door outside. What was the word for dust? I could say . . .

I forgot about all that. The hat was in my hands. It was like the chiffon cake at the bakery in Freiburg, all swirls and cream on a round piece of white silk.

At the mirror I put it on, dipping the front down over my forehead, using the white velvet band in back to keep it in place. Clever, that band. I had never seen anything like it. And the swirls, almost as if the ribbons had been let loose across the top and held down with rosettes.

I admired myself for the barest second before I took off the hat and examined that little band in back. I could do that; I could do better than that. Up close the stitches weren't nearly as fine as they should have been. Mama would snip them out and have us start over.

I took down the second hat. It was almost exactly

like the one I had made for Frau Ottlinger. I had to smile.

This was the America I had dreamed about.

In back of me the door opened and someone screamed.

I spun around, the chiffon cake hat still in my hand, the Ottlinger hat on my head.

It was Mrs. Koch. And even as I scrambled to put the hats back in the boxes, I tried to remember what *sorry* was in English.

And next came Aunt Ida, rushing up the stairs as if the French army were after her.

"In my dressing room?" Mrs. Koch said. "What? Who?"

And Aunt Ida took a deep breath, telling me in a fierce voice to go down to the kitchen while she explained.

Before I had been there an hour, I was sent back to the apartment and Barbara in disgrace.

Thirteen

"What is it?" Barbara asked. "Are you sick? Come inside. Tell me."

I sank into a kitchen chair, shaking my head, the Uncle's angry face in my mind. What would he say? And just as bad, the money, my savings that I had counted on for going home, had flown away.

Barbara brought me a glass of cold water with chips from the icebox. I gulped most of it down as I watched Maria in her high chair mimicking the face I made as I sobbed. She reminded me of Friedrich when he was a baby, mouth coated with cookie crumbs, laughing—a handful!

I'd never see Friedrich again, never see any of them at home again.

Through the archway into the hall, the sewing machine sat on the worn rug like a huge black beetle.

That was where I'd spend the rest of my life, and it was my fault, all my own fault.

I told Barbara the story of Mrs. Koch. "How was I to know I was in her dressing room instead of her bedroom?"

She didn't say, "You should have known." She didn't say, "You shouldn't have been in Mrs. Koch's closet anyway."

I hadn't told her about eating a little of the jam, which Aunt Ida had suddenly realized from a bit on my chin that I hadn't noticed.

And I hadn't told her that Aunt Ida had sat in the kitchen trying to catch her breath as I watched, thinking I'd have to send for the doctor.

"Do you know the word for *Doktor* in English?" I asked.

Barbara blinked and shook her head. "Are you that sick?" she asked.

She clucked over me the way Aunt Ida had clucked when she'd first seen me that morning. "I would have been terrified to try on the hats," she said, as if I had accomplished some brave feat.

I ran the cool glass over my forehead. It had been a long hot march back from Aunt Ida's kitchen.

"We'll take a walk," Barbara said. "We'll find the ice cream man and sit in the park. . . ." Already she was looking into her pocket, frowning as she pulled out a few coins.

I didn't know American money yet, but I could tell from her face it wasn't enough for all of us.

I shook my head. The coarse brown fabric was piled up on the chair in front of the machine, waiting for me. I'd have to begin now anyway. "Go ahead," I told her. "Take Maria." I waved my hand at the black beetle. "I'll sew."

To show her I meant what I said, I went into the hall, pulled out the chair, and began to pin a pattern to the fabric. I told myself I'd have to be starving in the street to wear such a scratchy thing.

I heard a banging at the door. *Now what?* I wondered. "Coming," I called. "Coming right now."

I could hear the Uncle roar. So he had heard about what had happened. How was it he was home in the middle of the day, though?

I took a deep breath and went to the door.

The Uncle was bent over almost double, and on his back and over his head lay piles of trousers. Dozens of them.

He straightened up, the trousers sliding onto the floor. He held up his hand. "You are nothing but trouble."

"Don't worry," I said. "If I ever get money enough, I will take the ship straight back to Hamburg. And from there I'll go to Breisach, even if I have to walk all the way."

"And worse than trouble," he muttered. "Always with the mouth."

I bit my lip. I remembered Mama shaking her head, telling me the same thing.

"Never mind," said the Uncle. "Now that service is out of the question, I have taken myself to Mr. Eis, who sells trousers."

I looked at them, a mound halfway to the ceiling.

"All you have to do is seam them together," he said. "If you begin every morning and work until dinnertime, we might get a dollar a day."

82

We. He had said *we.*

I began adding in my head.

"Seventy-five cents for me," he said, "twenty-five for you."

I opened my mouth. "Fifty."

"Don't forget. It is my machine, my thread."

"Forty for me," I said.

"All right," he said, almost smiling.

I had to smile, too. He had forgiven me for Mrs. Koch. And someday I would be going home to Breisach after all.

1 August 1871

My dear Dina,

I am taking a quick moment to write to you. I have been working on my trousseau with Mama and Friedrich: sheets and pillowcases with lace that we are crocheting by hand at night, petticoats with pleats and borders, . . .

We have discovered something. Friedrich has that magic in his fingers that you have. He sews beautifully, and better still, he loves it. Even at the age of ten he tells Mama that someday he will take over the business and she can rest and eat lemon cookies with Frau Ottlinger.

So it is Franz who now has the picture of the Fifth Avenue Hotel and Madison Square.

Krist sends his best to his "almost sister." And I send my dearest love to you.

Katharina

My dear Dina,

Last night I dreamed about you. You were laughing. It makes me happy to think that.

Love,
M.

fourteen

Everything ached: my feet, my wrists, my spine from leaning over the machine. But the worst was my neck. When I lifted my head to reach for another pair of trousers, I could feel a stabbing pain that began in the back of my head and went through my neck so that I wondered if I'd ever stand straight again.

But every stitch I took was one stitch closer to passage on a ship. Too bad I had no idea of the cost.

Each week the Uncle gave me American paper money, and I went straight to the trunk and tucked it behind the torn lining.

Barbara spent her days going from kitchen to roof, washing, then dragging baskets up to hang wet shirts and diapers. She swept the dusty apartment and cut vegetables for that night's supper. In between she did the finishing work on the trousers, sewing on buttons, snipping threads, or catching openings in the seams that I had missed.

At home that never would have happened. We sewed slowly and carefully, pressing each seam as we went along with irons that waited for us on the stove. But here everything depended on speed.

Barbara was the only one of us who seemed happy. Maria spent hours crying and throwing her blocks because her molars were coming in, and the Uncle spent his evenings taking over where I left off, yawning, his face determined and grim.

"Someday," he said to Barbara, "things will be different. I will have a shop and life will be easier."

I thought the same thing as I raced the machine down the long seams of the trousers: *Someday I will be home. I will open the door and there they will be, looking up at me, surprised. . . .*

Barbara smiled and nodded at both of us, then took five cents to buy a little green plant for the windowsill. "Watch," she told us. "It will bloom this winter. Better than anything else we could spend it on."

The Uncle and I looked at each other. For once each of us knew what the other was thinking. We even smiled, quick smiles. Neither of us would have spent five cents on a plant.

Barbara patted Maria, patted me, and patted the Uncle's head as he sat sewing. She even patted the leaves of the little plant.

And she sang, all day, every day. It was an American song about a small brown jug. And Maria and I joined in when she got to the part *Ha, ha, ha, you and me, little brown jug, how I love thee!*

Sometimes Kristel, the girl who lived downstairs, brought up coffee and small squares of biscuit, and we'd stop for a half hour, but most of the time Barbara and I were alone, bent over our work as Maria crawled through the piles of trousers that the Uncle brought home once a week. She threw her blocks or sucked on rags dipped in sugar to make her forget about the pain in her gums.

The piles of trousers never seemed to diminish. To get to the bedrooms, or the kitchen, or out the door, we had to climb over them.

And the Uncle rolled his eyes at me when I tried to speak English. "Kristel is teaching me," I told him.

"Kristel barely speaks English herself," he said.

I narrowed my eyes at him. When I reached home in Breisach, I would never speak English again! *Never!*

One afternoon, covered with bits of thread and lint from the fabric, I decided I had had enough. I finished the pockets on a pair of pants, pushed my chair back, and stood up, rubbing my neck and shoulders.

I looked into the kitchen. Barbara's hair was limp and her face shiny with perspiration.

I went in and stood beside her, moving her hands from her work. "Let's go for a walk. Let's sit in the park."

Barbara stood up and began to heat the flatiron on the stove, her hand on her back. "It's too much to get Maria ready," she said.

"I'll take her with me gladly," I said, bending down to look under the table as Maria peered out at me.

Barbara reached into her pocket. "Take a penny," she said. "Go for a walk. Go alone. You'll be able to do twice as much afterward for the rest."

I felt my face flush. How generous she was. But I was as worried about saving as the Uncle. I shook my head. "Keep your penny."

She smiled, though, and dropped it into my pocket.

I touched her shoulder, then brushed myself off, picked up the bottom of my skirt to straighten it out, and at the last minute went into the bedroom to put on my hat in case I saw the boy in the tailor shop.

Heaven! I had left the hat at Mrs. Koch's house and never even missed it.

I put on the other one, the one I had worn the day I arrived in Brooklyn, and went down the stairs. The door to Kristel's apartment, which she shared with her mother and four sisters and brothers, was open. I waved at her.

The door to the apartment below was open, too, and I peeked in. Dust motes and smells of old food and milk filled the air. The pan under the icebox had over-flowed not once but many times, leaving stains on the floor, and sometimes puddles that spread under the table. And today Mrs. Haberton lay on the sofa, her face red with fever. Her son bent over her.

I went by quickly, down the stairs and out the door. It was cooler outside, a beautiful fall day, with a sky so blue it almost hurt to look at it.

Homesick weather.

To make it even harder, I could hear women sitting out on their stoops talking. I could understand every word. Of course, they were speaking German. After all, as the Uncle had told me, many of the German immigrants came right here to this section of Brooklyn called Bushwick.

Two boys ran ahead of me, chasing each other, so

close to the dray horses clopping by that I raised my hand to my mouth. But after a moment they reached the other side of the street, safe. Laughing and pushing each other, they could have been my brothers. I felt an ache in my throat.

But after a few steps I told myself to stop thinking about home for an hour. I heard the whir of wings and looked up, shading my eyes. A streak of gray went by overhead: birds beating their pale wings against that blue sky. Pretty. I wondered what they were called.

The ice cream man's cart with its striped umbrella was just ahead of me. I could almost taste the cold drizzle of ice in my mouth.

Forget about home, I told myself. Forget about trousers with their four endless seams, their two pockets, their three buttons.

Forget about all of it.

With my carefully chosen ice cream, I sat on a bench, eating it as slowly as I could to make it last. Katharina would love it. I wondered why we'd never had it at home. Maybe because we were never outside at this time of day, always working in the sewing room.

A moment later the boy from the tailor shop sat down next to me, an ice cream in his hand, too. His teeth were white and straight when he smiled at me.

"My name is Johann," he said, wiping the drips off the side of his cup with one finger. "John now."

I didn't answer him. In Breisach I would never have spoken to a stranger.

"In America it's different," he said, almost as if he had walked into my brain and looked around to see what I was thinking.

I couldn't help smiling, but I kept my eyes down.

"Your name is . . . ," he began.

I took a taste of my ice cream.

"Hedwig?"

I shook my head.

"Anna Maria?"

Another shake. Another taste of ice cream.

"Juliana?"

I smiled. It was my favorite name.

"Ah, Juliana. That's my grandmother's name. She lives in Freiburg."

Freiburg. Grandmother's house.

I turned to him. Ice cream forgotten. Manners forgotten. "Where?"

"Water Street."

Not far from the Rhine. He knew the swell of it on a stormy day. He knew the barges, and the small birds that hovered over the water looking for fish. I rubbed my eyes with my thumbs.

"How long have you been here?" he asked.

I shook my head. "It seems like forever."

"Yes." He nodded. "I am here three years."

He was older than I. Maybe just those three years. I wanted to tell him about the terrible pains in my chest when I thought about Breisach, about how when I awoke in the morning I didn't want to open my eyes in such a strange place.

But I thought he must know it, too.

"And sewing . . . ," I began.

"I want to be a locksmith." His face lighted. "To make beautiful heavy keys, thick locks." He broke off. "And you?"

A locksmith, I thought, like Papa. "I don't want to sew, either." But then I thought about the hats I had made, the excitement of choosing fabric, the planning, adding lace, or flowers, or feathers. But that was different, not the same as the drudgery of the long seams, the endless hems, the boring pockets. Fashioning hats didn't count as sewing.

We were silent, watching the horses clop by, listening to the oompah-pah of the German band playing music on the corner. And then we saw a funeral carriage, its sides made of glass so we could see the coffin inside, and people walking behind.

"Dead from the smallpox, I guess." Johann turned toward me. "It's getting worse every day. The health department comes to knock on people's doors and take the sick to the hospital." He shook his head. "It's to stop the spread of the disease, they say, but most people who go to the hospital die, packed in tight with very little care."

I thought of the red ribbons Barbara and I had put around the apartment even though the Uncle said it was nonsense.

My ice cream was gone. The time had gone, too. I had to get back before the Uncle did, to make a dent in that pile of trousers that was waiting for me. I nodded at Johann; then I stood up and started down the street.

He called after me. "Come back tomorrow, Juliana."

I thought I just might do that. I might even tell him my real name.

fifteen

I saw the health department wagon in front of our place, the two men with their dark beards knocking on someone's door, just as Johann had said. I hurried past them, but one called after me. "Say hello to the little girl who waves at herself."

He meant Maria, I realized, but I was too afraid to answer. I took the stairs as quickly as I could, happy to see the apartment door. The Uncle was waiting in the hallway, walking back and forth.

"Dina," he said, sounding excited. "You're to come with me now, to Mrs. Koch."

My eyes opened wide. I never wanted to see Mrs. Koch or her beautiful house again. I felt my face flush every time I thought of that morning with her breakfast and the hats. But the Uncle was hurrying me out the door. I went past the kitchen first, seeing a plate of cakes on the table, and took one to nibble on as we went down the stairs.

"Does she ever stop eating?" the Uncle muttered to himself, taking enormous steps. "Mrs. Koch is waiting. Waiting for you."

Downstairs he stopped at the door, looking at me, shaking his head. "The cake."

I brushed the crumbs off my mouth and straightened my old hat.

"Your collar, not the cleanest."

I stopped there in the street, next to the building, and quickly unbuttoned the collar, turning it inside out. "What else?" I asked.

"I think that's all."

"What does she want, anyway?" I asked.

"Mrs. Koch does not tell me, and I do not ask," he said. "I take care of her horses, her barn, her garden. And that's enough."

Ten minutes later we were there, going up those steps, my hand on the railing, my pulse ticking somewhere in my throat. We stopped in Aunt Ida's kitchen while she went upstairs to knock on the parlor door to tell Mrs. Koch I was there.

The Uncle was already out the back door on his way to the garden when he turned. "Say yes, say no, and otherwise, don't talk," he said.

"You're making me nervous," I said.

"You don't know what it is to be nervous," he told me, but he was smiling just a little.

I tried to smile, too. "You're right."

"For once," he said, closing the door in back of him.

I didn't really have time to be nervous. Aunt Ida

came bustling back, tugging at my skirt, straightening my hat, my sleeves. "You look fine. Go into the parlor."

"Where . . ."

She rolled her eyes. "I'll take you, or you'll end up in a closet somewhere."

Upstairs, Aunt Ida reached out to knock, and then she was gone.

Mrs. Koch was waiting for me. I caught my breath. Dangling from her fingers was my hat. My pink hat with the droopy brim.

I looked from the hat to her face. I hadn't remembered what she looked like. It had only been a second or two from the time she screamed to the time Aunt Ida had rushed me out of there.

Mrs. Koch had a friendly face, with large dark eyes, and she wore a white lace morning cap over her faded red hair. Old-fashioned, those caps; only people like Grandmother wore them now.

She pointed to a chair and I slid into it. "Talk," she said, leaning forward. "Tell me about yourself."

And so I did. I told her the terrible thing I had done, I told her about Breisach and Katharina, and sewing, and a machine for straw hats. I told her about my river as it rushed along its cement banks, and König, my cat, and Franz and Friedrich. Mrs. Koch nodded all the while.

I stopped suddenly and closed my mouth.

"What's the matter?" she asked.

I swallowed. "I think I wasn't speaking English."

"No matter, I came from Heidelburg a long time ago." She waggled her hand. "You are speaking both, half German, half English."

"The Uncle said I don't speak well."

She laughed, leaning even closer. "I can just imagine. He's a little irritable."

Irritable. I ran my tongue over the word. I didn't know what it meant, but I liked the sound of it.

"Tell me about this," Mrs. Koch said, patting the hat in her lap.

"The hat?"

I was off again, speaking one sentence in my own language, supplying the few words I knew in English here and there. I told her about the hat I had given to Katharina and the pattern from Elise. I leaned forward to explain how I had snipped away the bottom drawer of the dresser, and as I told her, she reached up to take off her morning cap and put my hat on her head.

I stared at her, and then—how did I have the nerve—I moved forward to tilt the hat just a bit, fluffing the lace, and shook my head at her.

"What's the matter?" she asked.

"Wrong color," I told her slowly. "And the brim . . ."

She went to the mirror. "You're right about the color, but the brim is what makes this hat unusual." She twirled around. "How would you like to make me a hat just like this one?"

sixteen

Every day the leaves became more golden, the sky the color of fall: sharp blue, and cloudless. I found the materials for Mrs. Koch's hat in a store called A. T. Stewart, and used Elise's pattern, except that I formed the base with buckram, which was stiff but not so rigid that I couldn't bend the edges to frame her face.

I had to laugh when Mrs. Koch told me no one else would have a hat like it. Of course not, since the bent edges were a mistake.

It was such a happy week, working on that hat, finishing it, trying it on Barbara and then on myself.

I tried not to think about the smallpox disease that so many people in our neighborhood had. On one of my trips to the park, Johann told me some people were being vaccinated against it.

A strange word, *vaccination*. I nearly fainted when I heard it meant to puncture the skin with a needle filled with the cowpox disease. How terrible, even though I heard that the Prussian soldiers had all been vaccinated during the war.

One morning I awoke uneasily, thinking about the day ahead. The Uncle was leaving, driving Mrs. Koch in her carriage to a lake somewhere in New York. Even though it was out of season, she wanted to take the waters for her constitution. They would be gone at least a week.

Taking the waters I understood. In Baden, people took the waters all the time for their health. I wished Barbara and Maria could do that, too.

Maria had been sick for a few days, now her face flushed with fever, and the night before, Barbara's face had been red, too, her eyes heavy as she bent over the little girl, checking her arms, her legs, her stomach for signs of the pox. But "Nothing," she told me with relief. "Not one mark."

I dressed and went into the kitchen, planning my day: Run up a few pairs of trousers to make the Uncle happy before I began a second hat for a friend of Mrs. Koch. Sweep the apartment, which gathered grime from outside every moment. Go downstairs for water and wash Maria's diapers. It was going to be a busy day.

The Uncle was still in the kitchen, his hand on Barbara's hair, looking worried. The Uncle, worried! We could hear Maria screaming in her crib. She sounded very much like the Uncle. I had to smile. Maria was much more appealing than he was.

"I'll bring her a bottle," Barbara said.

"She is like you, Dina, that baby," the Uncle said.

And as I stared at him in shock, he sighed. "I must leave now."

He said goodbye to them in the bedroom as I took a scoop of the meltwater to give Barbara's plant a drink. I looked carefully for the buds that Barbara promised were coming, but all I saw was a sturdy green stem with a few pale leaves.

The Uncle came back to the kitchen and hesitated. "If something should happen . . . ," he began, "I will not be here."

I caught his eyes. "I will," I said.

He stood there, chewing the edge of his lip, and then nodded. "All right. I know you will do well facing trouble."

For a moment I couldn't move. I couldn't speak. It was the nicest thing anyone had ever said to me.

I listened to his footsteps going down the stairs and went to the bedroom door. Maria was asleep already. Barbara sat on the edge of the bed resting her head on the iron bars of the baby's crib, her eyes drooping, almost asleep herself.

I tiptoed in, touching her hair the way the Uncle had, moving her feet up onto the bed and covering her with the blanket. She nodded at me, whispering thanks, and I went back out to tackle the apartment.

The window over the air shaft in the kitchen was the worst. Nailed shut, it was always covered with an oily soot. I wondered what would happen if I removed the nails. Thinking about it, I went downstairs and lugged up the water, enough for a pailful of diapers and nightshirts.

I put the water on to boil and then I worked with one of the Uncle's tools to pry the nails out of the window. At last it slid open, letting in a whoosh of air, papers, and soot.

A terrible idea! But after a few minutes the dust settled and air came into the apartment, and as I bent over, scrubbing at the glass with a cloth, light!

I worked all that morning, stopping to look in the bedroom every once in a while. And later, I told myself, I would take a quick walk to the park, just once around and back.

I did that, and saw Johann at his table, bent over a piece of fabric, intent on what he was doing. I wished I had the courage to knock on the window or to walk by a second time, but I saw his father standing there looking out, and I scurried past, going home to Barbara.

On the way I saw the health department cart, the horses raising one hoof and then another as they waited for the men to carry out still another person on a stretcher. A person with smallpox, a person destined to die in the hospital.

I forgot about Johann then and raised my skirt to my ankles to run home. I never stopped until, breathless, I reached the top floor and our apartment.

I leaned against the door for a moment to catch my breath, then went into the bedroom. Both of them slept on, and as I tiptoed to the crib, I saw the first small mark on Maria's cheek.

That night, I stirred weak soup filled with vegetables and spooned it slowly into Barbara's dry mouth. I held a bottle for Maria to suck. She had several more pockmarks, and they were beginning to ooze. I washed her face gently with a soft rag, and then Barbara's, and at last threw myself on the sofa, still dressed, to doze.

seventeen

I was dreaming again. This time I could see my river imprisoned in its cement banks, gray and bleak. Great chunks of ice smashed into the stone bridge, jostling each other, squeaking and screaming, almost as if they were alive.

I knew I was dreaming and was angry that I wasn't imagining a summer river, with barges drifting along in the sunshine and sailors waving their ribboned hats at me.

I awoke to Maria crying in her crib again. Why didn't I hear the sound of Barbara's footsteps or her soft voice soothing her?

I lay there trying to clear my mind; it was as filled with cobwebs as the wooden steps in the cathedral tower. My eyes wanted to close, but I knew there was something I had to remember.

Just on the edge of my mind.

Slipping away like a chunk of ice in the center of the river.

I felt my head nod and realized: I lay on the couch, no covers, still dressed. I ran my fingers over the buttons, the top one open, my belt loosened. And then I was on my feet in an instant, stumbling over my shoes on the rug, running down the hall into Barbara's bedroom.

I glanced at Barbara in her bed, tossing and turning. Her hair almost covered her face, her head moved from side to side, her hands plucked at the blanket. She was muttering something under her breath.

But Maria first, Maria screaming in the crib, her red face a mass of raised pustules, her eyes and mouth swollen, her tiny fingers scratching at her cheeks and then her arms. I glanced at the red ribbons on the bars of the crib. How right the Uncle had been. They were useless.

I lifted Maria, wrapping the blanket around her, and sank down on the floor, rocking her back and forth. "Oh, poor baby, poor baby," I crooned.

I couldn't believe I had slept, couldn't believe I had closed my eyes.

"Dina," Maria was saying through her tears. "Dee-na." The first time she had said my name. Her first word, I was sure of it. I was filled with love for her.

"Bottle," Barbara was saying.

"I know," I said. "Don't worry, I'm here."

"Give her . . . ," Barbara said again.

"Yes." I nodded, but I wasn't thinking of Barbara's words but of Johann's: *Most people who go to the hospital die.*

I glanced at the small window over the bed. Light shone through; it was daytime.

Never mind wanting to sleep. My legs felt weak as

I thought of the wagon that would roll down the street in just a short while, the medical emblem on the side, the two health workers going from house to house, checking to see if anyone had the disease.

Smallpox. A word that seemed like nothing, but such a terrible sickness. If only I could pick up Barbara and Maria and take them somewhere, hide them.

There was no way to do that.

This morning, they'd take Barbara and Maria, and we'd never see either of them again.

How could I ever tell the Uncle?

Never mind the Uncle. I loved Barbara, with her sweet face and soft ways. I loved Maria, with her tantrums, and her block throwing, and her smile.

I put Maria back into the crib and went into the kitchen for the bottle. The tube down the center was coated with old milk. I worked at it, running some of the water that was left through it over and over, and in back of me I heard the water dripping into the pan under the icebox. If I didn't empty it soon, it would flood the kitchen floor.

All the time I was thinking about what I could do about the health department men.

I could show them a spotless apartment. Show them a spotless Maria, a spotless Barbara. For a moment I told myself it was too much, and what difference would it make? The men would take them both anyway.

Beg them, came a voice in my mind. The Uncle's voice: *Say please.* I practiced it in my head, and then aloud as I gave Maria the bottle.

"*Pliz,*" I said as I ripped up soft clean cloths and wrapped them around Maria's hands so she couldn't scar her face with scratching.

"*Pliz,*" I said as I washed her face and changed her diaper cloths, tucked knitted booties over her feet, and buttoned a clean white gown around her.

Pliz: a begging word.

And in back of me, Barbara called out, sensing that I was there even in her fever: "Hide the baby, Dina. Hide the baby."

I went into the kitchen and scrubbed the floor, put the milk back into the icebox, swept the hall, and changed my dress.

Pliz.

eighteen

I heard the cart, the horses clopping, the wheels grinding. I bent to look out the window. The cart stopped at the first house, leaving a trail in the mud behind it.

Still barefoot, I ran into Barbara's bedroom to slap her cheeks gently, and then a little harder. "Listen to me, Barbara, stand up."

Barbara's eyes stayed closed. "Dina?" she whispered. "Hide the baby."

I slid my hands under Barbara's back. How hot she was! I lifted her slowly until she was sitting, leaning against the pillow. Since I had thrown myself on the couch the night before, a mark had appeared on her forehead.

"We'll trick them, Barbara. We'll try." I reached for the brush and ran it through her hair: Barbara's shining hair, lank now, hanging in knots, damp with perspiration. How could I ever trick them?

I combed Barbara's hair into loops over her forehead and felt a quick rush of tears as I suddenly remembered Katharina standing in front of the mirror playing with her hair. It wasn't possible to hide the mark completely, but it was the best I could do.

From the window I could see the wagon moving again. I had time to wonder if someone had been taken from the first house as I slid Barbara's feet and legs from under the blanket. Marks there, too, on her ankles, but her skirt would hide them.

I rubbed her legs, wondering if I would come down with the pox. A stab of fear went through me as I thought about the men coming, pulling me out of my bed, dragging me down the stairs and into the cart on a stretcher, never to return from the hospital.

I dressed Barbara, listening to the soft sounds of Maria sucking on her bottle and the wheels outside in the street again. They were at the third house.

Barbara leaned against me. Her voice was a whisper, hard to hear. "Hide the baby."

I looked toward the crib. Maria, still awake, eyes unfocused. She'd be asleep in a moment. And even if I could hide her, what about the crib? What about the list the men might have telling who was in the house?

I walked Barbara into the kitchen, holding her tightly so she wouldn't fall, and pulled on her apron with its spicy smell of cinnamon. The downstairs door was opening now. Would they start at the apartment on the ground floor or would they come up the stairs and begin at the top? I could hear the rough feet on the steps below, coming higher.

We were next, then.

I looked down at my feet, remembering that my shoes were by the sofa. I leaned Barbara against the sink. "Can you hold on?"

"Hide . . ."

I curled Barbara's hands over the wooden rim of the sink. "Don't talk. Don't turn your head. Just hold on." I took a step away from her, hesitating, wondering if she could do it.

"Hide . . . ," Barbara began, but I could hear the noise of heavy footsteps turning up the last stairway. I pulled on my shoes, buttoning the bottom two buttons, no time for stockings, then went in to Maria, almost tripping against the sewing machine in my haste.

I pulled off the old blanket and kicked it under Barbara's bed with my foot, then covered the baby with a clean pink blanket, one I had stitched with rosettes in a pattern across the top the first month I had been here. How sad I had been as I had twisted the ribbon into tiny circles and cut snippets of green for the tiniest leaves.

Would the men be rough with Maria? Would she awaken and begin to cry when she saw those strange faces?

I felt fear in my mouth and my throat, my tongue so dry I could hardly answer as the men pounded on the door.

"Coming. I am coming, sir." But I knew they couldn't hear my whisper. I walked slowly down the hall and opened the door for them.

They came inside, those big men with dark beards, so big they seemed to take up the whole room.

At the sink Barbara's head was lowered, her hair a

veil over the side of her face. Her hands were slipping off the sink and I took a step toward her, leaning against her for just a moment.

One of them motioned to her with his thumb.

"No English she speaks," I said. "Greenhorn."

They both laughed; I knew it was because of my own English. But that was all right, as long as they left her alone and didn't make her turn toward them.

"Is there sickness in the house?" one of them asked.

I betrayed Maria with a quick look back down the hall.

They brushed past me and I followed them, standing in the doorway as they looked down at her.

"The baby who waved at herself," one said. "Such a pity."

"*Pliz.*" I grabbed his arm, almost forgetting how afraid I was of him. I held tight. "We will take care. Her mother and I. The apartment is . . ." What was that word? "Clean. Is so clean. The baby is clean."

He turned to me and shook his head. "We have to . . ."

I raced on. "She will die in the hospital."

The man raised his hand and uncurled my fingers from his sleeve. "She has the pox. I'm sorry. I'm so . . ."

A voice came from the kitchen. Barbara.

"What is she saying?" the man asked.

I didn't bother to answer. "*Pliz.*" I was wringing my hands now, blocking the doorway. "We will not move out of this house. We will stay in here with her until she is better or . . ." I was silent then.

They glanced at each other, one of them flipping his finger across the red ribbon. They were sorry for us.

But in the end I think it was not I who saved Maria.

She awoke suddenly and looked up at the men and smiled, her small shy smile, the most beautiful smile. I could feel it myself, the sweetness in it, even through the redness, the oozing blisters. Maria, our tyrant!

She raised one little hand in its white cloth, almost as if she'd give them a backward wave; then her hand fell and she closed her eyes. I went to the crib and put my head down on the crib rail, hearing the soft sound one of the men made in the back of his throat. "Like my daughter," he said gruffly. "No one sick here. A clean house, good careful people."

They tramped down the hall again, through the kitchen, not even noticing Barbara as her hands slid away from the sink. They had just closed the door behind themselves when she collapsed on the floor in front of me.

nineteen

A week later, in the middle of the afternoon, the Uncle arrived home to find us all asleep, Barbara and Maria in the bedroom, me dozing with my head down on the edge of the sewing machine.

Barbara heard the door close and came out of the bedroom with Maria in her arms. "Lucas," she said. "You are home."

He looked from one to the other. Barbara's eyes were huge in her pale face, her hair in a braid down her back, and she was leaning against the wall for strength. Maria was a mass of thick scabs, and it was already apparent that she'd have several pitted scars on her cheeks from the disease.

Lucky, though; she was alive. Lucky they were both alive.

The Uncle gathered them into his arms; then, carrying the baby, he guided Barbara into the kitchen to help her into a chair. He turned to me. "And you, Dina? Sleeping in the daytime with all your energy? Are you sick, too?"

"No." I shook my head. "I'm fine." How could I say how tired I was! My legs trembled with fatigue at times as I walked endlessly back and forth at night holding Maria, her arms wrapped around me. I hummed the lullaby Mama always sang, that beloved song, with tears in my eyes for Mama, but loving Maria, determined that she be well.

How could I say that my days were spent helping Barbara bathe and cleaning the dust off the chairs, the table, even the beds? I knew now it was a mistake to have opened the window over the air shaft so that every bit of soot and paper flew into the apartment.

I was tired, too, from running up the long seams on the trousers, and my knuckles were bruised from the finishing work on that coarse material. The week had gone by so quickly, I had spent almost no time working on a new hat for Mrs. Koch's friend.

I was tired, but not sorry!

I went back to the sewing machine and slid in the next two pieces of fabric to be hemmed, half listening to the Uncle as he talked about all he had seen on the way to Lake Placid. "Mountains," he told Barbara, "not unlike the ones in Breisach. Gentler, though. And I saw a tailor shop, talked to the man who owned it. It wouldn't take much to do the same thing here. . . ." He broke off. "The window is open."

"So it is," Barbara said, noticing it for the first time.

I began to sew, the noise of the machine drowning out what the Uncle had to say next.

It didn't drown him out for long. In a moment, he

was calling in a voice that I could have heard even on the roof. "Dina!"

I didn't move.

"Where are you?"

I looked up at the ceiling.

"Dina!" he shouted again.

I sighed and got up from the machine to go into the kitchen. "I was suffocating."

He shook his head. "I thought you were going to take care of everything here."

I narrowed my eyes at him as Barbara began to talk, to change the subject, while he reached for the hammer to close it again. "I dreamed when I was sick," she said. "So many dreams."

"Fever dreams," he said over his shoulder. "Terrible, I know."

"Yes." She ran her fingers along her braid. "I dreamed I was back in my house as a little girl. I dreamed . . ." She smiled at me. "I dreamed of Dina, who washed and dressed me."

She stretched out her hand. "I know you did that for both of us."

The Uncle put down the hammer, the window back in place, shut tight; no more grime to come in, and no more air, either. He nodded at me. "I'm grateful for that, Dina."

I didn't know what to say, but Maria was holding her arms out to me, so I took her from Barbara and balanced her on my hip, rocking just the slightest bit.

"I dreamed that men were in here," Barbara said. "Men with beards like the giants from one of the Grimm brothers' tales."

I ran my fingers along Maria's neck, making mouse

feet for her. Barbara was right. The men had looked like giants with their black beards.

"I dreamed . . ." Barbara closed her eyes. "Dreamed that I was telling Dina to hide the baby, hide the baby. . . ." She opened her eyes, hesitating. "That was the worst dream of all."

"Never mind," the Uncle said, pouring thick hot coffee from the pot on the stove. "It was just a dream."

I bent my head. "Mousie creeps," I said to Maria, making her smile again.

17 September 1871

Dear Dina,

Krist and I were married yesterday. It was a beautiful ceremony in St. Stephen's Cathedral, with Krist smiling at me all the while. The whole town was there, dressed in the finery that we had sewed. I carried the beautiful hand-kerchief you made. And afterward we had coffee and cake and small candies wrapped in foil.

The only sadness was that you were not there, my dear sister, and at the moment the church bells pealed out with joy I thought of you and how much you mean to us. I wonder if you could feel our love across the waves.

All love,
Katharina

Dina, my child,

You would have loved this wedding. Katharina's dark hair looked beautiful under her hat. We covered the wide hat frame with the same gray silk as the dress, adding two large plumes of white, which covered the rim. We spent hours on the dress, as well, pleating the entire bodice and finding the perfect piece of lace for her neck. If only you had been there to take those fine stitches of yours!

I love you, Dina.

Mother

Twenty

It was growing colder by the day. I took time to make myself a muff from a small piece of velvet I had found in the Uncle's pile of fabric. I stuffed it with cotton and tucked my hands into it when I went to the park to meet Johann.

"But today it is too cold to stay outside," he said.

I nodded, disappointed. I thought of not seeing him for the rest of the winter and then reminded myself I was going home one day; better not become too fond of him.

It was hard not to, though. His hair curled down over his forehead, and there were just the beginnings of a dark beard over his lip and his chin.

"There is a bakery nearby," he said. "It is owned by people from Freiburg."

"Really?" I said, digging my hands deeper into the

muff, hunching my shoulders just a bit against the wind as we walked. "Brooklyn is everything the most," I said.

He stopped, his hand on my elbow. "What does that mean?"

"In the summer it's the hottest, in the winter, the . . ." I searched for the word.

"Coldest," he said. "But never mind, we will go to this bakery and sit at a table. We will have chocolate and cookies and I will teach you English."

"Do you know it that well?" I asked.

He smiled. "You will not know the difference," he said.

We hurried along, laughing, and slipped into the bakery, where the air was steamy, the chocolate lightened with cream, and the cookies still warm. The Black Forest clock ticked over the counter, the minutes passing quickly as I learned words from Johann and forgot them two minutes later.

He told me more about wanting to be a locksmith, and I told him about Papa. I told him about Mrs. Koch's hat, too, and he said the strangest thing. "Your eyes light up, Dina, when you talk about making the hat."

"I don't like sewing," I said.

"I think you do." He popped the last of his cookie into his mouth. "I think there are parts of it you love."

"Not those long seams," I said. "Not the sewing machine. Not the plackets, the zippers . . ." I hesitated, thinking about the hat that was half finished, a flat plate of rose petals shot through with green velvet ribbon. "But the hats . . ."

"You see?" he said, laughing, and reached across to touch my hand. His hand was warm, and I could feel my face begin to flush.

We finished our chocolate, then went back out to the cold again. There was a pale sun over the houses, softening them. And the bare branches made lacy patterns against the walls. I could hear the German band playing even on such a cold day.

I left Johann at the park and went on to our street, feeling strange inside. What would it be like to go home, I wondered, and never see Brooklyn again? What would it be like never to see Johann again?

Twenty-one

Blossoms of ice coated the air shaft window, and the first snow had settled in the streets. My hands were chapped and cracked from hanging wash on the roof and then taking it down, dry but stiff and crackling with frost. I made sure that I was the one to do that chore; Barbara's time was coming soon. Weeks, maybe, or even days.

Excitement was everywhere. Christmas was only days away.

Whenever Maria slept, I worked on her doll. Johann had found a small porcelain head for me, and I had fashioned a soft cloth body for it.

Every spare moment, I cut tiny petticoats and dresses with aprons to match for that doll. I remembered when I was small Mama had given me a doll with clothes in a small wooden trunk.

One morning I reached behind the torn lining in

the trunk for a bit of my precious money and took myself down to A. T. Stewart's to buy a few feathers, a yard of crimson ribbon, buckram, and felt.

The money would double itself, triple itself. I had just gotten orders for three hats to be delivered two days before Christmas, the loveliest to Mrs. Koch, of course.

In the evenings Barbara and I baked Christmas cookies that we formed into wreaths and snowmen. I teased Barbara, saying she was like one of those plump little snowmen herself with her round cheeks and her apron tight around her middle, smelling as always of the cinnamon she carried in her pocket. How lovely she looked standing there laughing, her hands covered with flour.

I couldn't think about that, though; I couldn't think about Barbara's needing me. By next Christmas I'd be home. If only I could wrap all this up and take it home with me: the steamy kitchen and its trays of cookies, Barbara handing me one to try, Maria on the floor banging her shoe so loudly and grinning up at me, pleased with herself.

"One day," Barbara said, reaching out to touch my arm, a dusting of flour on her chin, "we'll fill your trunk with sheets and pillowcases, and petticoats with edgings that we'll crochet, and . . ."

"Foolishness," the Uncle said, but I could almost see the curve of his mouth as he smiled under his beard.

"In the meantime," Barbara said, "it will be Maria's second Christmas. Dina and I will bake fruitcakes, and we'll light the rooms with candles everywhere."

Next Christmas, flickering candles in all the windows in Breisach, the lights reflected in the river.

And then at last the holiday was on us. Mrs. Koch

sent an armful of evergreen branches that had been cut for her in Lake Placid to put on our mantel. Barbara and I took deep breaths. "It smells like home," she told me, taking my hand and doing a little dance down the hall with Maria following us, grabbing us by the skirts until Barbara lifted her and danced with her.

On Christmas morning, we all went to church, walking slowly because Barbara tired easily now. I looked at the women's hats and bent my head, telling myself not to be so vain. But none of the hats was as pretty as the three I had made for Mrs. Koch and her friends. And none was as lovely as the one Barbara wore now, with the leftover feathers and crimson ribbon, the felt brim dipping low over her forehead.

I was conscious of Johann and his family sitting in the pew directly in back of us. I sat up straight, glad I had taken time to sweep my hair back with clips. I noticed that Johann had a strong deep voice when we sang the hymns and had to keep telling myself to pay attention to the priest.

I smiled, thinking about the lovely days when we walked through the park and the cold ones when we sat in the bakery. He often talked about the promise his father had made to set him up in a corner of their men's shop. "One day I'll make a key just for you, Dina," he said. "The only one like it."

We laughed over this language we were learning and tried to outdo each other with strange-sounding words.

"Do you know what *Schlamm* is in English?" he asked.

"Ha, of course. It's *muddah*."

He laughed. "Say *mud*. No *ah*."

"I like it better with the *ah*," I said.

We leaned forward, our heads together. "Muffin. Puff pastry," he whispered.

"Yes, puff!" Wonderful on the lips.

We'd leave each other smiling, marking the time until we saw each other again, calling back: "Sunrise, sofa . . ."

Then it was Christmas night. I opened my trunk and tucked away the blue striped scarf Barbara had knitted for me, and the small sewing wife with its needles and pins and silver thimble from the Uncle. I stopped to look at the candles on the mantel and the windowsill. In the dim light, everything glowed. Shadows patterned the walls and the ceiling. What a beautiful day it had been. Dinner with everyone around the table, and Aunt Ida telling us that Peder had written saying that next year they would surely be together.

I unbuttoned my shoes and eased out of them, then suddenly remembered the wash. I had run up to hang it on the roof yesterday. Another night up there and everything, chemises, nightgowns, diapers, would be covered with soot . . . gray forever. "I'm just going to bring in the diapers," I called in to the kitchen.

"Oh, Dina," Barbara began. "Never mind. It's late."

I didn't answer. I let myself out of the apartment, not bothering to put my shoes back on, holding the wash basket against my hip, and ran up the stairs to the roof on tiptoe, pushing open the door and hearing the wind banging it shut behind me.

I glanced at the sky, which was filled with stars and a dusty moon, and took a step forward in the wind. In front of me, one of the diapers blew off the line and sailed off the roof just ahead of my grasping fingers.

Shifting from foot to foot on the icy rooftop, I looked down over the edge to see the white square gently fly across the street like a kite and land on a step.

I hadn't bothered to put on my coat, either, so I was cold standing there on the windy roof, brushing my hair out of my eyes, but the sky was so beautiful I was in no hurry to go back to the apartment.

Below, people still hurried along dressed in festive clothes. A few women wore old-fashioned hoops that sailed up in front as the wind caught them. I leaned against the wall, sheltering myself from the wind, peeking down at them and at the candles that glowed in the windows across the way.

People were pointing at something, perhaps at our building, but I couldn't see what it was. A Christmas tree covered with small candles, or the wreath on the door?

I remembered a blustery afternoon hurrying along the Schwartz Street in Breisach, opposite the black-smith's shop. It had been so cold I had crossed over and walked through his open doors to gather warmth from his enormous fire. Standing near his forge, watching him pump the fire with his bellows, I had breathed in the smoky odor that surrounded him.

Why was I thinking of that now? The cold, but something else. The smell of the smoke from his fire. I could smell it here, too. Wisps of it came from every chimney.

Taking my time, I began to pull the wash off the line, dropping it and the clothespins into the basket: Maria's small stockings, her slips, her nightgowns, not much bigger than the clothes of the doll she had loved when I gave them to her.

I had a secret. Under my shirtwaist was a key on a

chain. It was slim and lovely, with the tiniest red stone in the center. Johann had slipped it to me after church, unwrapped. *"Merry Christmas,"* he had whispered.

"Merry Christmas," I had whispered back, proud that I knew the words. I had clutched the key so tightly on the way home that it had left marks in the palm of my hand.

If the Uncle ever found out, he'd tell me to give it back. I rubbed my feet against each other in my woolen stockings, thinking Mama would have a fit that I had accepted anything from a boy.

I finished with the wash at last and took one more look over the edge of the roof. More people had stopped, a knot of them huddled on the corner, the wind blowing through them so they had to hold their hats and skirts down.

Something felt wrong to me, and I remembered the blacksmith again. Strange; I could still smell his great forge and the smoke that swirled around it.

I spun around on the roof. Was that it? Smoke? The licorice smell of fire? And then I saw them, curls of gray coming from under the metal door.

I was instantly seized with fear. Through my mind went the memory of the small mice that sometimes scurried along the riverbank at home, their eyes dark with terror when they saw me. Once I had been so close to one that for a second, the small creature had been unable to move. I had stood still, too, and then he had darted first one way and then another to escape the huge creature in front of him.

I was doing the same thing.

Twenty-Two

I began to move, first back toward the door, feeling the heat of it against my hand. Too hot to open. How had this happened so quickly?

I went one way and then the other along the edge of the roof. Had the air shaft window been open, I could have let myself down that one story. But some-one down below saw me. Face upturned, he cupped his hands against his mouth. "Don't go back into the building," he called. "Candles in the first-floor apart-ment caught fire. It's a powder keg now. Use the side stairs."

Behind me, the door burst open with a great roar and flames shot across the roof, sending fire to lick the tar and ignite the wash in the basket.

My heart pounded in my chest and in my ears as I scrambled over the hot tar to the stairs with the black wrought-iron railing that snaked its way down the side of the building. Terrified of the height, but more afraid of the fire, I threw myself over the side of the wall and onto the steps. They moved with me, the metal warm against my stockinged feet. I could hear someone screaming and realized the sounds were coming from my own mouth.

But then I had no breath left. What came into my lungs was searing heat, and I flew down that uneven stairway, jumping the last few feet into the arms of that kind man who had told me the way down.

I ran toward the group of people who were gathered on the corner under the streetlight. Kristel, the girl from the apartment below ours, sat on the ground holding two of her brothers by the hand, her hair snarled and down to her waist, her legs bare, her shoes unbuckled on her feet. Her mother was there, too, her shawl over her head; her hands, pressed against her cheeks, were trembling. Their faces were black with soot. The woman from the first-floor apartment sat in the filthy street, hunched over, rocking back and forth, dazed. "My fault," she said. "The candles were too close to the curtains. My fault."

My hand went to my mouth. I turned, twirling in the windy street, looking for Maria and Barbara and the Uncle. Not there. Still in the house, then.

In front of me was the door to the building. I reached down. *"Please,"* I said, and took Kristel's shoes off her feet. "I have to . . ." I pointed. "My family . . ."

My family. It was the first time I had thought of them that way.

Kristel's head was on her raised knees, her hair covering most of her skirt. "What are you doing?" she asked.

I crushed my feet into the shoes, which were much

too small, wondering if I could get through the front door, hearing the sound of bells in the distance—not church bells, perhaps a fire engine coming with water.

I was through the door in an instant, looking up at the stairway, which seemed to be covered in a dense fog, like the bridge over my river on an early spring morning. But this narrow bridge that led upstairs had tongues of fire running along the banister and across the top two steps.

I put my hand in the band of my skirt, not bothering to unbutton it, but pushing out as hard as I could so the buttons popped. . . . Mama's voice was in my head: *Dina, always you make the buttonholes too wide*.

I stepped out of the skirt and the petticoat Barbara had spent hours trimming, two pools of fabric to burn on the bottom step.

I saw Mama's face. *What will people think?*

I took the stairs two at a time. My head felt fuzzy now. I was coughing, trying to find breath.

By the time I reached the top step of the first floor, I could feel the heat through Kristel's shoes and on my legs. And as the banister turned onto the second floor, through the smoke, I could see Barbara, almost a shadow, and behind her, guiding her with one hand and holding Maria in his other arm, was the Uncle. The bottom of Maria's blanket was smoldering.

Steps above me, he leaned over the banister and put the baby into my arms.

I turned, went down the steps, down, toward the door. Maria was still sleeping, had slept through all of this; otherwise why would her eyes be closed, and why would she be so still?

I reached the door with a man guiding me, such a large man, and I remembered vaguely that I had seen him sitting on the steps next door during the summer. Then I sank down into the street with the baby in my arms.

A voice that sounded like Mama's said, "Did you see that? Did you see what she did?"

And I realized she was talking about me.

Twenty-three

In my dream I swam in the river, diving deep into the water, sounds echoing around me, a school of fish and a ship gliding past above me, and then someone moaning. Was it Barbara? It seemed that Aunt Ida was saying, "Ah, I know, I know."

I was alone in Aunt Ida's kitchen, I thought. But the blur of water covered me and I floated, eyes closed.

Later I heard another voice. "Gone. Everything gone."

It seemed as if I were in a tunnel now, with voices bouncing off one wall and onto another.

A baby was crying. Was it Maria? But this sound was the sound of a newborn child, high and weak.

I opened my eyes and felt with my hands under the thin blanket. My own clothes were gone. I was wearing a huge cotton nightgown.

And how hard the bed had become, reminding me

of the hot nights I had slept on the roof upstairs. Then something tugged at my mind. The roof. What had the blacksmith been doing on the roof? How did he breathe in that forge of his?

I shook my head. I was dreaming, half asleep, half awake. And then I remembered. The fire.

I tried to sit up, but it was hard to move, hard to breathe.

"You've slept most of the night and most of the day," Aunt Ida said.

I turned my head. I could see a corner of the parlor, two stippled walls, two chairs.

"The other way, Dina," Aunt Ida said. "Look here."

I turned back to see her sitting there and realized I was on the floor with a blanket folded underneath me. "Barbara?" I asked.

"In the bedroom."

I ran my tongue over my lips.

"She's had a baby, Dina, a boy."

I struggled to sit up, feeling a knocking in my head and a sudden surge of sickness coming up from my stomach. "Is everything all right?"

"A fine baby," she said. "Ernest, after your grandfather. And Maria is in the kitchen with Lucas. She's all right, too, not a burn, not a mark."

Alive, then; all of us alive. I raised my hand to my head, feeling the pain in my fingers, seeing the strips of cloth that covered my arm from wrist to elbow.

"It's not a bad burn," she said, "but still, I've covered it with lard."

I nodded, and before I was even sure I was thirsty, she was off the chair and bending over me, holding my head up so that I could sip from a cup of cool water. I swished it around in my mouth. Had I ever tasted anything so good?

I gathered the blanket around me and went to stand at the bedroom door to see baby Ernest. He had a small fuzz of hair on his head, and his face was red from the effort of crying, waving his fists in the air.

I went into the room to lean over him, and put my mouth on his forehead, the skin wrinkled and softer than anything I'd ever felt before. I touched his chin, his shoulders, his fists, and it seemed as if he stared up at me, knowing who I was. And I knew who he was, all of us in our family, my grandparents, my mother, dear Papa. I felt as if I'd never loved anyone so much.

Next to him, Barbara smiled at me, her eyes filling, too. I watched them: tears drying on Barbara's cheeks, the baby's fists relaxing and falling to his chest. And in my mind I heard Barbara's voice again, *Everything gone*.

Not everything.

But I thought then of my suitcase with the pink lining, the money for home, my clothes, even my shoes. Every trace of home, so many things Katharina and Mama had made for me.

And what about the Uncle's fabric? The pile of trousers for the man at the shop? Would we not have to pay for them? I tried to get the words out. "Cloth" was all I could manage. And then I had an even worse thought: what had happened to the sewing machine, the black beetle?

"Sleep," Aunt Ida said. "We will worry later."

How strange—sun was streaming in the dusty window. It was daytime. I went back to the parlor dragging my blanket. I was going to sleep as if night had just begun.

Ernest was crying again; the cry wove itself into my dreams, and Maria's coughing, as well. When I woke again, at last, it was afternoon. It had begun to snow. A soft gray light filtered through the window. I sat up to see the three of them sleeping in the bed in the corner. Barbara was in the middle, her arms around Maria and the baby.

On the floor next to me was a neatly folded pile of clothes. Underwear, a waist and skirt, wool stockings, and even a pair of worn shoes.

I put everything on quietly, wondering what had happened to Kristel's shoes.

"Thank you for the clothing," I said to Aunt Ida when I reached the kitchen, "but where . . ."

"Mine," she said. "Are you awake? Feeling better?" She waved her hand. "A stitch here and there, a snip of the scissors this morning. You are just half my size." She smiled. "The size of the shoes is . . ."

"Fine," I said. I leaned over to give her a kiss. "I want to go back and see the apartment."

"Don't do that, Dina," she said with a quick shake of her head. "Let it be."

My eyes were brimming with the thought of the apartment on Christmas evening, filled with candles, soft in that light. "I have to," I said, and she patted my shoulder with her warm hand, sighing. "That's what Lucas said."

I let myself out the door and went down the stairs. Outside, the flakes were large, covering everything: the lights had small caps, and the steps clean new pillows of snow. I turned the corner, hurrying now.

When I reached our street, I could see there were gaping holes where windows had been, and great patches of black covered the building. In front of me were piles of wood and rubble.

Others had had the same idea I did. People picked through the charred remnants on the first floor, people who hadn't even lived there.

I went inside toward the stairs, wondering if they would hold me. Treads were missing, and the banister looped over the steps. I looked up, fingering the sides of my skirt, and behind me someone said, "Don't try it, miss."

But suppose something was left? Something I could bring Barbara or Maria.

And underneath it all I was thinking of the money tucked behind the lining of my trunk. Suppose that heavy wood had withstood the fire? Suppose I could put my fingers inside and find my money, neatly folded?

Home.

Bent almost double under a beam that seesawed over the banister, I started up. Smoke still swirled on the high ceilings, and everything was warm to the touch. I pulled my skirt higher, and holding on to the side of the wall rather than the banister, I eased my way from one step to another, feeling my own unsteadiness and the unsteadiness of the stairs themselves.

I stopped where the Uncle had handed Maria down to me and saw that a small piece of her blanket had caught in the banister, blackened, almost like paper. No one would have recognized it as the soft pink shawl Barbara had knitted, leaning over in the dim light in the evenings.

The next flights were easier, not that they were in better condition, but I knew now how to use my shoulder against the wall, the hand that wasn't burned against the tread itself. Like a small spider I went up.

When I reached the top, I saw our door half open. The rug with its poor bare spot under the machine had burned away. But the machine was there, a melted ruin, and so was the Uncle. He was leaning over it, crying.

The Uncle. Crying.

I took a step backward, and another, and rounded the top step so he wouldn't know I was there. But in my haste I touched something, the edge of the banister, perhaps, and one of the posts detached, falling through the opening to the next floor, and the next, hitting everything as it went, making a tremendous clatter, raising smoke and dust, and causing someone below to call, "All right up there?"

The Uncle turned as I went toward him, staring at me, surprised, his eyes red, but I might not have known he was crying if I hadn't seen it.

"What are you doing here?" His voice was shaky. "You climbed the stairs? What is the matter with you?" He was like the Prussians: attack, attack. Always I had to defend myself.

I shook my head, running my hands over the machine.

"Foolish," he said, as if he hadn't done the same thing, maneuvered those stairs to see.

My mouth was dry. "My money, all in the trunk."

I walked past him, glancing in at the kitchen. Bags had sprung open, and flour and sugar were mixed together, gray and grainy on the floor.

And then my own closet bedroom: the mattress sagging and dark, the trunk closed in front of it, covered with soot and patches of black, and pitted in spots.

I sank down on the floor to run my hands over the metal strips, and opened the trunk to see nothing: clothes gone, lining gone, money gone, all of it just a layer of ash on the bottom.

I knew I'd never go home. Never see the house in Breisach, or my family. Never.

Everything gone.

I rested my head on my knees. This was the worst moment of my life, worse than the soldiers at the river that day, worse than saying goodbye, worse than the terrible trip with the storm and my terrified prayer that I'd never eat again on Good Friday if only we survived.

I don't know how long I crouched there, but then I remembered the Uncle. I went back to stand in the hallway, seeing that the machine belts had burned and snapped, and the piles of trousers and fabric were completely gone, as if they had never existed. Like my clothing. Like the lining and my money.

"Will you have to pay the man for the trousers?" I asked slowly. Even talking seemed an effort.

He didn't answer. He was down on his knees now, his head tilted, trying to see if he could repair it.

Of course he'd have to pay for the trousers.

And the fabric. The fabric that had belonged to him, that would start his business; that terrible scratchy wool, the lengths of cotton. I remembered that I had taken enough for a dress for myself without thanking him. I had never paid him back for it.

I bent down next to him. It was no use. The sewing machine that I had hated was gone along with everything else.

"I was going to go home," I said, hardly realizing I was saying it aloud.

We left an hour later, with no energy to talk, but the mailman came running after us waving a letter from Katharina. I knew it would be her Christmas greetings. How strange. Christmas seemed such a long time ago.

1 November 1871

My dear Dina,

How busy we are you can imagine, but Friedrich and Franz are helping greatly. Everyone is thinking about winter and the holidays coming. I think that by the time you receive this it will be Christmas, so I send you the happiest of Christmas greetings.

At last that terrible soldier has gone. Krist spoke to him and says he will never come back.

I, too, am thinking I might have a wonderful surprise. It is too early to tell yet, but Krist and I are hoping that we will have an announcement to make very soon.

Much love,
Katharina

Happy Christmas, dear Dina.
Friedrich and Franz send kisses, and I also.

Love,
Mama

Brooklyn

1872

Twenty-four

On New Year's Day, we sat around Aunt Ida's table, crowded together, Ernest in my arms and Maria bouncing on my feet as if I were a *Wippe*. Ah, *seesaw*. I'd have to tell that odd word to Johann.

I smiled, looking at the baby, counting in my head. I was sure Katharina was hinting at a baby for her and Krist, probably to be born in the summer.

In front of us was all we owned, things the Uncle and I kept bringing home. A few spoons and forks, a rolling pin with one burned handle, a tin of needles and pins, the pots and pans that just needed scrubbing, and, strangely, Barbara's apron. It had hung on a hook in the kitchen yet was barely singed.

Aunt Ida moved the coffeepot from the stove and poured cups for all of us laced with sugar. "And a dollop of whipped cream for comfort," she said. Because there wasn't room on the table for the raisin cake just out of the oven, we held the warm pieces in our hands.

We sat without speaking for a while, Maria pinching my ankles, trying to make me laugh.

I looked around at them, rocking the baby gently: Aunt Ida with her heavy comfortable body and soft face; the Uncle, his face smeared with lard, his eyebrows gone, his beard ragged, his hands black, and both arms still covered with cloth.

Deep inside me a small voice: *Not the worst, Dina; oh no, not the worst thing in life to be here with people you love, and yes, who love you.* And something else, which Johann had whispered to me after church on Christmas morning. *Don't ever leave, Dina.*

My hand went to my neck to feel the chain and then the slim key under my shirtwaist. *Johann.* I pictured him bent over his table fashioning the key for me. I pictured his hair falling over his face. And then I thought of him laughing and how I loved to make him laugh.

But these were fast thoughts, fleeting thoughts, because I realized everyone was staring at me. I raised my hand to my face, feeling where my eyebrows should have been, and my hair singed at my temples.

"Never mind," Aunt Ida said. "It will all grow back."

And then the Uncle spoke; his voice was the way it always was, almost challenging me to disagree with him. "I have decided something today," he said.

I took a sip of the coffee, wondering what was coming next. He was frowning, and Aunt Ida turned away to put the pot back on the stove.

I thought he was going to talk about the trousers, or the machine, or even the fire itself. I glanced at Aunt

Ida, then at Barbara, and could see they knew what he was going to say.

"I am sending you home, Dina," he said. "You will be in Breisach by spring."

I sat there, the warm cup in my hand. I opened my mouth but I couldn't speak. Inside my head was a picture of my river, my bedroom on the third floor, Mama's face, Katharina's, my brothers laughing with each other at the kitchen table. The joy of it!

And then I realized why he was sending me back. I had not fit into this family. They didn't want me. And why should they? For the first time, I thought about it. Every word I had spoken to the Uncle had been angry or irritable. And still another thought. I looked up at him. "But where will you get the money?"

He patted his waist. "It is always with me in a little bag. You don't think I'd be foolish enough to put it in a trunk."

"Lucas," Barbara said, and he was quiet.

"I'm sorry," I said. "It is my fault that—"

The Uncle's eyes gleamed. He didn't wait for me to finish but spread his hands wide. In a husky voice so unlike his, he said, "I would never have gotten Barbara and Maria around the stairwell and down the last flight of steps. One of them, perhaps. But both, never. Barbara's skirt had already caught the flames, and Maria's blanket was scorched."

Next to me Aunt Ida began to cry silently.

"If you hadn't . . . ," he began, and stopped.

And Mama's voice in my head, *If you hadn't forgotten the bread rising . . .* How far away Frau Ottlinger seemed. How far away the sewing room, how far away Breisach.

127

"How could we keep you here, knowing how unhappy you are?"

He knew. He had known it all along. And now I was crying, like Aunt Ida. "But the money . . ."

He looked down at his hands. "The sewing machine is gone. The fabric. The trousers for Mr. Eis."

I was nodding. "So I can't take the money."

"You don't understand," he said. "What is gone is only a foolish dream. My work for Mrs. Koch is good. I like rubbing down the horses in the warm sun. And Mr. Eis . . ." He hesitated as if he were thinking it through. "I will pay him back little by little from my salary."

It would take him years; it would take him forever. But I had never heard him talk so much in all these months. I remembered his crying and how proud he was. "I can't," I said.

"You certainly can," he said. "It is what I want."

Had I ever won a battle with the Uncle? "Thank you," I said, looking from him to Barbara, hardly able to get the words out. "But if you do this for me, I will pay you back someday."

We sat there for another few minutes drinking coffee. Suddenly I felt so tired; it was an effort to raise the cake to my mouth. I felt my head drooping, my arm throbbing.

"Sleep, Dina," Aunt Ida said.

I touched the baby's soft hair and gently slid my feet out from under Maria. Then I put the baby into Barbara's arms, and went back to Aunt Ida's bedroom.

I wouldn't see either of them grow up; they wouldn't even remember me. But I'd take home a picture of them in my mind. I slid into bed thinking about all I'd have to tell Mama and Katharina.

And Johann. I'd have to tell Johann.

My dreams were strange, dreams of the bakery shop burning in a fire and Johann bent over a key, dreams of Maria asking me for another doll. "Go home," someone said. And I kept whispering, "Where is it? I don't know where it is."

Twenty-five

Within a week we found an apartment, this one without even a closet for me. I would sleep in a space under the kitchen window. Barbara looked at me with brimming eyes. "I'm so sorry," she said.

"It's only for a few weeks, after all," the Uncle said. "As soon as the weather warms, you will take the ship."

I didn't mind the kitchen. It was a cold January, and it would be the warmest room in the apartment. The window faced the backs of the buildings across the yards, and there was always something to see: people calling out to each other, and children playing on the fire escapes. Sometimes, I thought, Brooklyn was an exciting place to be.

We planned to move on a Sunday. The Uncle would be home from work, and so would Aunt Ida. "Everyone will help," she said.

There was so little to move, though, I wondered why we'd need help. But on Saturday afternoon, Aunt Ida came home laden with things from Mrs. Koch: old sheets and pillows, three blankets, a waist and skirt for Barbara. And I ran to Schaeffer's shop to ask Johann to help, too.

On moving day, we told ourselves we'd manage to get the iron bedsteads down the stairs of our old apartment. None of us mentioned that we'd just have to leave the sewing machine.

We made a fine parade going to the new apartment. Someone had sold the Uncle old mattresses for a few cents, and he and Johann carried them on their heads. I carried Mrs. Koch's things, and Aunt Ida dragged Maria's iron crib along the street as Barbara came along at the end carrying Ernest and holding Maria by the hand.

Upstairs, Johann looked at the apartment. And as everyone scurried back and forth to put things away, we were left alone in the hallway.

"The apartment is very small," he said.

"But . . . ," I began.

"But . . . ," he said at the same time, "someday things will be different."

I nodded. It was time to tell him I was going home.

"My business will be a success," he said. "And when that time comes . . ."

I looked at him, shocked. *When that time comes . . .* I knew what he meant. My mouth was so dry I couldn't speak. How could I tell him my news? What could I say?

I didn't have to say anything. *"Success,"* he said. "How do you like that word?"

"Seesaw," I said, and then, before I could stop myself, *"Sorrow."*

At that moment, the Uncle came to thank him, and I watched as he went back down the stairs, taking the steps two at a time.

That night we looked almost as dirty as we had the morning after the fire. We sat in the kitchen spooning up Aunt Ida's vegetable soup and biscuits, feeling satisfied with what we had done, and talking about how we'd find enough money to live now that we owed Mr. Eis so much.

We tried to plan how the Uncle would tell Mr. Eis, talking it out at the table. And early the next morning, the Uncle put on his hat, straightened his collar, and went out. He was back an hour later, running up three flights of stairs to tell us: "We have an extension."

A new word to tell Johann. *Extension.* But what did it mean?

"Mr. Eis will give me a few weeks to pay him," he said.

"A few weeks?" Barbara said.

And I echoed her. "Only a few weeks?"

We sat there in silence, the three of us, Maria teetering on a chair, leaning against the windowpane until Barbara stood up and scooped her off.

"How could we possibly . . . ," Barbara began.

"We can't possibly . . . ," I said at the same time. And then it came to me.

"Suppose," I said slowly, "we spent the ticket money." I was surprised at myself for saying it, but strangely, I wasn't sorry.

Already the Uncle looked angry. "That we will not do."

"Suppose," I began again, "we bought fabric for a dress, for two dresses." I dared to look across at him. "Fine fabric. The best."

They were all looking at me.

"I will make two dresses from Frau Ottlinger's pattern, two beautiful dresses, and we will sell them to Mrs. Koch."

"Who is Frau Ottlinger?" Barbara said.

I waved my hand. "There's a pattern in my trunk. . . ." I bit my lip. "I know the pattern by heart anyway," I said, wondering if that was true.

The Uncle was looking at the ceiling. "To put the savings all into two dresses . . ." Then he snapped his fingers. "But yes, I can see it. You can certainly sew. You have a gift for it."

A gift.

"If we can sell both," I said, "we can pay Mr. Eis back for the ruined fabric."

"Yes. And still have enough for your ticket."

Yes. A few weeks more here. I wouldn't be sorry for that. I'd have time at the bakery with Johann, time to play with Maria and Ernest, time to cook with Barbara. Time to stay in Brooklyn.

Time.

And then the Uncle's face fell. "What are we talking about? We have no machine."

"For this I won't need a machine," I said. "I will do it all by hand, lace inserts, covered buttons . . ."

"Yes," he said, tapping my shoulder as hard as Maria usually did, and was gone, hurrying to his work in Mrs. Koch's house. "I will ask Ida to speak for us."

Barbara and I waited breathless the whole day, boiling Ernest's diapers, sweeping the apartment, running down to the store for a penny's worth of soup greens for a stew to simmer on the stove.

And then at last we heard Aunt Ida's footsteps on the stairs. She was lugging Mrs. Koch's cloth bust with her. "One dress," she said. "If she likes it, two."

We were jubilant. Barbara and I danced around the kitchen table, and I picked up Maria to dance with me. "*Good*, Dina," Maria said, hands on my face. "*Very good.*"

Aunt Ida gave me a worried look. "You'd better be sure you can do this, Dina."

The Uncle and I went to A. T. Stewart's and pored over the fabric and trimmings. We spent exactly half of the ticket money for the makings of the first dress. I smiled, thinking how lucky we were that Mrs. Koch was half the size of Frau Ottlinger.

"Smiling is not good," the Uncle said, "when everything rests on this."

Quickly I put on my most serious face, even though I was more excited than I could say. I pointed to a bolt of cloth called Old Rose, the most beautiful piece of silk I had ever seen. I turned my head to see it change color in the light: one way it was a shimmer of soft gray, another it was pink. And through all of it was a thin line of green that wandered across the fabric like a tender vine.

I was almost ready to begin. But first I rubbed my fingers together. My skin was dry from the fire, the cuticles rough. If I even tried to cut or sew that fabric, there'd be pulls from one end of it to the other.

I went to bed with gloves over hands slathered in lard. And the next morning I walked around with my fingers in the air, touching nothing, even though I knew the Uncle was becoming desperate with my time wasting. I did take a few moments to write a quick note to Katharina, not mentioning the fire or coming home. One was sad, the other to be a happy surprise.

That afternoon, I washed my hands under water without soap until every trace of the grease was gone, and my fingers and palms felt soft again. I took pattern paper we had bought from A. T. Stewart's and I began to shape the pieces with a pencil.

I reminded myself of the dress Mrs. Grant had worn

when her husband had become president. I had studied that picture in the newspaper and knew I could make a dress very much like hers. I began to cut, marking the pattern for diagonal bows. It was almost as if I were back in Mama's sewing room and sure that she would help if I ran into any trouble. "It will be a dress with a short waist and a bustle with narrow ribbons in the back," I told Barbara as she leaned over my shoulder. "A dress that even a president's wife might wear."

I took the fabric from its paper wrapping then and shook it out, a beautiful tent of cloth to spread across the kitchen table. I looked at that silk. What would happen if I made a mistake? There were no second chances. And what would happen to us if I ruined it?

And all the time I was thinking of the sewing, the French seams with edges folded over on themselves, the stitches, each one the size of a tiny seed.

And something else. Mrs. Koch loved hats the way I did. I'd be careful with the cutting, and there might be fabric left over, bits and pieces that I could shape into flowers for a hat that would go with the dress. Surely Mrs. Koch would buy that, too.

Suddenly I realized I was humming. And Katharina's voice came into my head: *Dina's happy, she's making bird sounds.*

Coo-coo, Friedrich would have said.

I began to arrange the pattern over the cloth one way and then another to save as much of the fabric as I could. Then I picked up the scissors and began to cut.

Twenty-six

If.

If I hadn't learned to sew.

If I hadn't left my hat at Mrs. Koch's.

If I hadn't found the most perfect Old Rose fabric.
So many ifs.

I took the dress over my arm for Mrs. Koch's first fitting and slipped it over her head in her dressing room. We looked in the mirror together and caught our breath.

"I've never had anything so lovely," Mrs. Koch said, admiring the delicate pleats in the bodice, the circular arrangement of the material I had swept up for the bustle.

I knelt on the floor with pins in my mouth the way I used to in Mama's sewing room, mumbling through them that there would be a hat, as well, and both would be finished—I closed my eyes for a moment—within the week.

I'd stay up all night if I had to.

"March," Mrs. Koch said dreamily. "Spring."

"Excuse me?" I said, the thought running through my mind that I had said the words almost the way an American would.

"Everyone will be wearing straw hats," Mrs. Koch said. "I've seen the advertisements in the newspaper, but nothing like what you could do."

I could see the hat in my head, a straw base, flower buds made from the silk. But then I shook my head. "Straw . . . ," I began.

"You said that your sister wrote about a machine," Mrs. Koch said.

"Expensive," I muttered, thinking that we didn't even have the black beetle anymore. And then I took a breath. "If," I said, not even realizing I was talking aloud as I helped her slip the dress off over her head.

"If . . . what?" she asked.

"If I weren't going home . . ."

"Home?"

"I'm going back to Breisach," I said. "It was never my dream to come here and sew. Sewing is my uncle's dream."

She sank down on her pouf of a chair, still in her chemise. "You foolish girl," she said, sounding just like the Uncle. "A dream! A dream is nothing unless you can make it happen."

I began to fold her dress.

"Your dream is to sew," she said.

"No, never."

"Well, let me say it this way. This is your talent, like it or not. This is what you should be doing."

Mama. She sounded like Mama. I wrapped the dress in a sheet.

Mrs. Koch reached out and took my arm. She held it hard. "I will buy the machine. You and Lucas will pay me back a little at a time."

I kept shaking my head as Mrs. Koch turned to put on her morning dress, and smoothed down her hair. She reached into her dresser drawer and pulled out some money. "I will pay you for the dress and the hat now," she said, "more than you asked, because, of course, you will make me another, and still another. And more for my friends. And someday, you will have more work than you ever dreamed of. You have a wonderful future."

"Thank you," I said, laying the dress over my arm to be hemmed, "but there will be only one more dress before I leave for Germany."

She shook her head impatiently. "Take the money," she said. "You've earned it."

Outside, it was a beautiful day. Soon the Uncle would buy me the ticket. I'd be on my way before the heat of summer. But for the first time I thought about that terrible trip, that long way, so far I'd never come back to America again.

I went past the park to Johann's shop and saw him bent over a table in the corner, working on a key. I stopped, trying to remember something. And then it came to me. I had dreamed of him just there, and in the same dream I had been lost, looking for home.

I tapped on the window and he came outside, squinting a little in the bright sunlight. "Christina Dina Bina," he said, smiling.

And then I began to blurt it out, all of it. And while I did, we walked toward the park and sat on a bench.

I told him about the Uncle and the ticket. I told him how much I missed my family. I told him what Mrs. Koch had said.

"Breisach," I said. "I am going home."

"Home is here," he said, reaching out to me. "Look at the people walking in the streets, all from Germany or Ireland or some other country. Every one of them homesick. All of us, in the beginning. And sometimes now even I miss Freiburg. But oh no, Dina, you belong here. Everyone needs you. And I . . ."

Before he could say more, I stood up. I could hardly see him for the tears in my eyes. "I must go back to the apartment now," I said, "before the dress becomes dusty."

I went down the street listening to him call after me: "Stay, Dina. *Stay.*"

I passed the flower shop next, and bought a small flowering plant for Barbara to replace the one that had been lost in the fire. Not such a foolish thing to spend money on a small plant, I thought.

Back in that tiny apartment I put Mrs. Koch's dress carefully on the bed while Barbara was exclaiming over the plant. I put the money into her hand. "It's yours," I said. We stood there for a few moments, and she reached out to hold me. "Dear Dina," she said. "You are my dearest friend."

I spent the next hour bent over Mrs. Koch's dress, sewing tiny stitches in the wide hem. And when I was finished, I embroidered my name under the collar: *Dina Kirk.*

I sat there looking at it, proud of my work, remembering Mama did the same thing. *Frau Kirk and Daughters.*

And at the same moment, I felt as if my heart

would burst. I wanted to go back. I wanted to stay. I belonged in both places. I put my hand on my chest to still the pain, felt the key.

I couldn't bear to leave them all: Barbara, Maria, Ernest, and even the Uncle. I couldn't bear to leave Johann. And it was true. I *was* proud of my work, and maybe that was just as important as loving it.

And something else. They needed me, and deep in my heart I knew that it would be hard for them to manage this new venture without me. What could be more important, I thought, than being needed?

Dear Mama. Dear Katharina. Dear Franz. Dear Friedrich. I love you all. I will miss you forever.

I sat there for a long time crying for them. Then I wiped my eyes and stood up. There was something I had to do.

Twenty-seven

"A festive dinner," Barbara said, "with pork and noo-dles, and Aunt Ida brought apple strudel."

The Uncle had counted out all the money, telling me there was more than enough to pay Mr. Eis and buy fabric for the second dress. "And with that," he said, "comes your ticket."

I didn't answer; I waited until we had almost fin-ished dinner before I began, and then, almost trem-bling with excitement, I asked, "*Dear* Barbara, could you live in two rooms in back of a shop?"

"I could live anywhere," Barbara said.

And then I turned to the Uncle. For the first time, I was going to win a battle with him. I was like a Prussian sol-dier. "There's an empty shop next to Schaeffer's," I said.

"Empty since the Frohlings went down to Varick Street in Manhattan and took a train west," Barbara said, cutting into the strudel. "Can you imagine?"

There was a bubbling in my chest that came up into my throat. "I saw the owner today. It's for rent at a very low rate." I swallowed. What did I know about low rates or high rates or any rates at all?

The Uncle was eating strudel, hardly paying attention to me. Maria, my hat over her head, was tugging at him, wanting a taste of apple.

"I told the owner to hold it for us, that Lucas wanted to rent it." I wanted to look up at his face, but I didn't have the courage.

For one more second there was silence. Then he smacked his hand on the table. "Where is your head?" he asked.

"The ticket money," I said, and slapped my hand on the table as hard as he had. "I'm not going home," I said, and then, not being able to let go of it entirely, I went on, "Maybe someday, somehow. But don't you see? I can begin to sew in a shop. Soon we'll have enough money for a machine. Mrs. Koch offered to help. You and I will have a business together."

There was silence. Then Barbara pushed her chair back with a crash. "You are not going home! Oh, Dina!" She came around to my side of the table and hugged me so hard I didn't get to see the Uncle's face. I heard him mutter, though, "That girl. That girl. What will she do next to me?"

"If . . . ," I said to all of them, suddenly worried, "if you want me to stay."

"Ah, Dina," said Barbara, and Aunt Ida reached out to pat my hand, smiling. But it wasn't until later, much later, that I heard what the Uncle had to say.

Ernest had begun to cry then, and Aunt Ida, after more hugs, remembered she wanted to be home before dark, and Barbara suddenly went into her bedroom, telling me over her shoulder that there was a letter from Katharina. "I put it away for you," she said, going into her bedroom, "and almost forgot."

It was time for me to take down the wash from the roof. I tucked Katharina's letter into my pocket and went up with the basket. At the wall that ran around the edge, I stopped to look at the bowl of sky lighted by a full moon.

The tiniest square of the East River far along the edge of Brooklyn was visible between two buildings, reminding me of the ship I had taken, that endless trip.

When I closed my eyes, I could almost see the shop next door, and the small section where Johann was making beautiful locks and keys. I couldn't wait to tell him.

Johann Schaeffer, who sometimes called me Juliana, and sometimes Christina Dina Bina. I thought then about being here, about going into the stores and understanding what people were saying.

I looked out at the city and thought about wrapping my arms around it. I was beginning to love Brooklyn, with its heat and its cold, its dust and its dirt. I thought of Breisach, that beautiful festive town with its river and its cathedral, and knew I'd always be homesick for it. That was the price I'd have to pay, the same price everyone who came to this country might have to pay. At least I thought that was what Johann had meant: we would always have a longing to go back, and a longing to stay.

Katharina's letter was in my pocket with all her news from home. I'd wait until I'd folded the wash, savoring the thought of opening that envelope and seeing her small square letters. And maybe this time she'd tell me about the baby she had hinted at.

I began at the far end of the wash line, dropping the pins into the basket, folding Maria's small flannel sheets, Ernest's cotton diapers. Suddenly the door to the roof opened. It was the Uncle. He stood there looking over the city as I had. At the clop of horses, he said, "The health department wagon. Not frightening anymore. The fear of the smallpox is over." He hesitated. "I often wondered, Dina, was it a dream Barbara had about the men coming?"

I pretended I didn't know what he was talking about. I leaned over to flatten the mound of wash in the basket.

"Did you save them that day?"

I smiled. He didn't have to know everything. "A dream," I said.

"I wanted to tell you," he said, and hesitated, choosing his words carefully. "I remember something about my sister, your mother."

I wondered if I would ever stop missing Mama.

"*If,*" the Uncle said. "She was always saying that."

If you hadn't forgotten the bread . . .

"I'll say just this," the Uncle went on. "If you hadn't come . . ." He stopped then, and I could see he couldn't talk.

But what he had said was enough. More than enough.

"Thank you," I whispered.

He went downstairs then with the basket, and I stayed to read Katharina's letter, to hear her news at last.

5 December 1871

Dear Dina,

I think it's time for you to know our surprise. Krist's dream, like mine, has always been to go to America. So my dear sister, we are sailing on the S.S. Bremen late next month and should be there by April.

And maybe, just maybe, we'll be able to send for Mama and Friedrich and Franz someday. Wouldn't that be something?

I will look for you at the port, and together we will shed oceans of tears as we hug, this time for joy.

All my love,
Katharina

Darling,

Katharina says she will be wearing your hat. Of course!
Mama

AFTERWORD

As a child I loved stories my mother and her mother told about my great-grandmother Dina: a loving, laughing woman who bore fifteen children in eighteen years, and who was the heart of our family even long after her death. When I began to write, I always thought I'd write about her someday. Much of this is fiction, of course, but her spirit is real, I hope.

In 1870, my great-grandmother Christina Schütz, called Dina, took the terrible journey to America to escape sewing. When she arrived, she saw the rug worn bare and knew she had come to a house of tailors. She stayed with the Uncle until she married Johann Schaeffer. They suffered through the smallpox epidemic; the story of the health department is true, except it was Johann who cleaned the house and dressed Dina and her tiny baby, Mary. He convinced the men to leave Mary there, and as they left, Dina collapsed at the sink.

Mary carried the marks of smallpox on her face all her life, but she was loved by two men, her husband and his brother, both of whom thought she was beautiful.

The story of the storm on the ship was also true. For the rest of her life, Dina never ate or drank on Good Friday in gratitude for surviving it.

Katharina never came to America. She had a fine tailoring business and remained single all her life. Sadly, it is believed that as an old woman she was put to death by the Nazis.

The Schütz house still exists, not in Breisach but in Heidelberg. I have stood there several times looking at the Neckar River and remembering that every fall Dina would sigh and say it was homesick weather.

I write this especially so that the story of Dina and her beloved, Johann, will be remembered by our family.

Patricia Reilly Giff is the author of many beloved books for children, including the Kids of the Polk Street School books, the Friends and Amigos books, and the Polka Dot Private Eye books. Several of her novels for older readers have been chosen as ALA Notable Books and ALA Best Books for Young Adults. They include *The Gift of the Pirate Queen; All the Way Home; Nory Ryan's Song*, a Society of Children's Books Writers and Illustrators Golden Kite Honor Book for Fiction; and the Newbery Honor Books *Lily's Crossing* and *Pictures of Hollis Woods*. *Lily's Crossing* was also chosen as a *Boston Globe–Horn Book* Honor Book.

Patricia Reilly Giff lives in Connecticut.